TRAVELER'S CANDLE

by the same author

COAT FOR A SOLDIER

Florence Maule Updegraff

Traveler's Candle

ILLUSTRATED BY EVA A. WATSON

NEW YORK

HARCOURT, BRACE AND COMPANY

To MY MOTHER

*because she too has been
a Traveler's Candle to so many*

CONTENTS

TRAVELER'S CANDLE

1

THE HOUSE OF THE TRAVELER'S CANDLE

MISTRESS MAPES laid the candle wick she had just finished twisting onto the completed pile on the table before her and drew her shawl closer about her shoulders with a shiver.

"Seems like it's grown a lot colder since we started work," she observed, waited a moment for either of her companions to reply and, as neither did, looked from one to the other to see if her remark had been noted. Her face wore an expression of hopeful expectancy and her tone suggested the comment had been made trusting it might draw forth some desired response. But none was forthcoming.

Her young daughter seated across at the opposite side of the table seemed too deeply absorbed in measuring wick to notice. Her husband, perched on a high stool before a work-bench along the wall with his back to her, appeared entirely engrossed in the task of threading wick into one of a row of big pewter candle molds lined up on the bench in front of him. His back looked completely unresponsive.

It was a gray September day, desolate and chill. But the door and window holes of the room in which they worked were open nevertheless, so the indoors was as cheerless and cold as the world outside. Mistress Mapes suppressed a shiver and reached for another wick. As she did so her glance fell on her daughter again. The corners of the girl's mouth were twitching and a mischievous light danced in her eyes. When they encountered her mother's gaze she broke into a peal of merry laughter in which, after a dubious moment, her mother joined her.

"Very well, Mistress Hannah," the older woman said with the chuckle of a good-natured person who can laugh at herself, "thee wins thy point. I admit I should not have insisted on having the door and all the shutters open on such a day as this. Go close them now—e'en though it will make the room so dark for our work."

Hannah bounded off her stool as though shot with a spring. "That I will, Mother—and quickly before thee has time to change thy mind. I'm near to frozen."

The man had turned round to join in the laughter. "And me the same, daughter. But since thy mother was willing to near freeze herself the better to help with the chandlering it ill behooved the chandler to complain."

Mistress Mapes looked from one to the other with an expression of fond indulgence. "Foolish creatures, the two of you. I should let you freeze for your folly. Instead I'll go now and mend the fire so you can warm yourselves."

She rose and crossing to the big fireplace which nearly filled one end of the room began raking the embers together to coax them into a blaze.

Hannah ran lightly from one window opening to the other, swinging shut the wooden shutters hinged at their sides. There were six in all and no glass covered them. They were just square holes cut in the rude board-and-batten walls. They could be closed against the cold only by the

4

solid wooden shutters—and when those were closed they shut out all the light as well.

There was one window in the room, however, which did have glass in it. It was a tiny affair set rather high in the same wall with the door and recessed a little as though to protect the precious diamond-shaped panes leaded together to form its small rectangle. Very little light came in at it really. Not only because of its small size but because the glass was so cloudy, filled with flaws, and so greenish that it made light shining through it look as though it were coming through water. But in spite of its shortcomings, the little window looked actually elegant in comparison to the rest of the room which was furnished rather for use than appearance and evidently served both as the chandler's workshop and the main living quarters for the family.

When the girl had closed all the shutters and reached the door she paused to lean out and peer up at the gray September sky hanging low over the wooded hills that encircled the hilltop on which the house stood.

"I declare," she exclaimed, "it looks as though 'twere making ready to snow."

Mistress Mapes straightened up, poker in hand, and looked over her shoulder with a startled expression. "Mercy me, I hope not—with the bayberries not gathered yet and just right for picking."

"We'll get no snow for a month yet," the chandler reassured her. "But, beyond doubt, 'twill be raining by nightfall."

Hannah drew in her head, closed the door hastily, and turned back into the room remarking, "And a bitter cold rain 'twill be, too. I'd have no desire to be out in it."

5

Mistress Mapes turned round to answer, but when she noted the twilight gloom which had fallen on the room with all the openings closed she seemed to forget what she had intended to say and instead complained with a sort of bitter triumph, "Now look how dark it is! On such a day as this our window is near as good as none."

Her husband gave her a conciliatory smile. "Have patience but a bit longer, wife. When our candles are sold, I plan to go to Newport and get glass sufficient for three of the holes at the least."

But the assurance seemed unconvincing. "So thee has said each fall these many years past; but our candles have ne'er brought enough to reach to the glass. I doubt not but that we'll put oiled paper in the holes for the winter this year as always." She took down the candle holder from the mantel-shelf and lighted the candle at the blaze that had sprung up from the embers she had raked together. "Well," she added in a tone of long-suffering patience as she started back to her place at the table, "we'll have to finish our day's work by candlelight."

The chandler placed his hand over a spot just at the bottom of his waistcoat, cocked his head to one side, and seemed to consider some matter of great import. "Something here inside tells me 'tis nearing the hour for our evening meal. So why not declare blind man's holiday and stop work for the day?"

The expression of discomfort on Mistress Mapes' face changed as though by magic to a look of happy housewifely concern. "To be sure," she agreed, starting back to the fireplace. "I'll get the fire to going in good earnest and start the meal." She set the candle on the mantel-shelf and reached into the wood-box for a log to lay upon the blaze. Her hand groped vainly and she clucked her tongue with annoyance. "Now, as I live, if that heedless Jonathan has not gone off again without filling the wood-box. There's but one insignificant log left in it."

Hannah paused hopefully halfway back from the door. A trip to the woodpile would make an acceptable break in the monotony of a long day spent indoors. "I'll bring in wood to fill the box, Mother," she volunteered.

Her mother laid the last inadequate log on the fire and turned to answer, her face set in lines of determination. "Thee will do no such thing," she declared. " 'Tis thy brother's duty to fill the wood-box and he must be taught to do his stint. Throw on thy cape rather and run down to the top of the river path and call. I venture he'll be down at the river fishing again." Then turning to her husband, she continued, "I tell thee, Joshua, 'tis beyond me to know what to do with the lad. He's so fair daft for fishing."

But Joshua seemed entirely undisturbed by Jonathan's lapse from duty. "There, there, Mother," he protested mildly. "Thee must admit our fare profits greatly by what he catches." He paused, looking at her a moment with an expression of whimsical interrogation before adding with a chuckle, "I had rather fill the wood-box myself and have the fish."

Mistress Mapes gave a dry little laugh. "So the boy knows, all too well—and advantages himself of the fact. But he must fill the box himself each day—fish or no fish. So run on now, Hannah child, or the fire will be out ere he gets here."

Hannah needed no more urging and ran quickly to get her cape. She was starting for the door again when her father spoke her name in a loud whisper and beckoned her to him mysteriously.

The girl crossed to him, her face lighted with a knowing little smile.

Joshua laid his finger to his lips, nodding toward his wife as though in warning. "Bring back thy brother," he said in an audible whisper, "but first make sure he has a catch of fish."

Hannah bent close to him pretending a furtive glance at her mother. "Thee can count on me for that, Father," she whispered back in the same manner.

Mistress Mapes looked on with feigned disapproval. "I hear you plotting," she told them with mock sharpness.

It was a game they played in the household, Joshua and Hannah pretending to be in conspiracy against Mistress Mapes' discipline, and she making a great show of severity which deceived no one. So the affairs of the house went forward amid a gentle, playful make-believe.

As the girl stood beside her father the likeness between the two was striking. Both were slight and delicately built. Both had glossy chestnut hair and the same clear, hazel eyes like limpid water that looked out with an untroubled directness and seemed to have a light burning behind them. Both had an expression of whimsical gentleness and gave an impression of quiet like a deep, silently flowing river.

Mistress Mapes looked comfortably substantial and homely by comparison. She was plump and rosy. Her step was brisk and her manner purposely matter-of-fact and positive. But, in spite of her great display of domestic discipline, good humor and kindliness shone on her face and an unbounded affection for her family looked out of her warm brown eyes.

8

It was evident she really enjoyed the part allotted her in the game of her husband and daughter, for there was a twinkle in her eye as she watched them and her voice was merry as she admonished Hannah at length. "Come now, child, have done whispering with thy father and go and fetch thy brother."

Hannah skipped across the room, light and quick and quiet as a little ground-squirrel. With her hand on the latch she paused to throw back a parting smile to her parents.

Everyone who knew the girl watched for that smile. Its radiance seemed a lavish gesture of giving in which she bestowed upon others some portion of the light that glowed within herself. When she went out and closed the door behind her it was as though she had taken some of the light from the room with her.

Outside on the door-stone she stood a moment to draw her cape about her and let her eyes rove lovingly around the restricted circle of the landscape. Under the lowering September sky the great trees on the hills that surrounded their hilltop looked taller and appeared to be drawing together in an austere, waiting silence. She had heard people say the hills looked forbidding on such a day—but she loved them even so. Still she was glad their house was not hemmed in close by the woods as were many of the homes in those densely timbered hills of Rhode Island. For then you weren't able to look around. It was better to live on a cleared hilltop as they did, so you had what people called a "look off."

Their cleared hilltop was large enough not only for the house but for a garden, a barn and barnyard, and even a tiny orchard. Beyond that the woods crowded close. In

9

front of the house the hill slope had been cleared enough so you could see to its base. And there another wall of woods began.

A narrow trail emerged from the solid phalanx of forest and zigzagged up the hillside, passing the house and disappearing over the hill's crest. It was only a narrow, deep-worn path hardly wide enough for a single horse to follow in comfort. But Hannah regarded it with great respect for she knew it was one of the few means of land travel in that part of the colonies. It connected the Massachusetts Bay and Plymouth Colonies with Connecticut, traversing a large part of Rhode Island as it went.

No one knew how old it was. It had been worn there by the Indians during the hundreds of years they had walked single-file through the forest. The Pequot tribe of Connecticut had used it particularly as a means of reaching the eastern seashore. So it was called the Pequot Path.

Westward, over their hillcrest, it led to the Seekonk River, the little new settlement of Pawtucket, and then on to Providence. Hannah had been that far with her father when he went to deliver candles in Providence. But the chandler's business did not take him eastward, so she had never been farther in that direction than the foot of the hill. She knew, however, that the outpost villages of the Plymouth Plantation lay beyond the woods and that beyond those were miles of scattered settlements, then the seacoast with the big towns of Plymouth, Boston, and Salem.

She did not feel cut off from the life of well-settled districts by the wilderness that lay between. The trail brought it to their door. In fact, the little thatch-roofed house of unpainted clapboard perched on its isolated hill-top was itself another sort of outpost of that civilization. Hannah felt its importance keenly, and, as her gaze followed the twisting course of the trail down the hill and wandered off across the treetops of the forest, her face glowed with pride.

Hundreds of people off there beyond the woods knew about their house. Hardly a traveler started out upon the difficult overland journey from that comfortable, well-settled territory to the wild, new country of the Providence Plantation without being told about it.

"Should nightfall catch you ere you reach Providence," someone would say, "you'll find a house some five miles this side of Pawtucket where folks live that set out the traveler's candle."

Most people, in those days of the late sixteen hundreds, understood what was meant by the saying. But sometimes a stranger who did not know the ways of the country would be puzzled by it. Then it would be explained to him that a traveler's candle was a token of hospitality. In newly settled territory, where there were no inns as yet, certain households more kindly and considerate for their fellow man than most, set a lighted candle in a window that could be seen from the trail each night when they went to their beds as a sign their latchstring would be out and any passing wayfarer was welcome to come in and sleep beside the hearth.

The Mapes house was the only one for many miles along the trail that offered such hospitality, and Hannah regarded the setting of the traveler's candle as a sacred duty. She knew the candle had burned in the one glazed window of the little house even before she was born. In fact that the window had been put there in the wall fronting the trail for that very purpose. Her father had brought the precious glass for it all the way from Boston when he and his young wife had sought refuge in the Providence Plantation back in 1659 when persecution of folk of their faith had begun in the Puritan settlements. For Joshua Mapes and his wife, Naomi, were what people commonly called Quakers—though they themselves seldom used the term but spoke of themselves as Friends or Members of the Society of Friends.

When Hannah was just old enough to understand, her father had told her the story of how it had come about that he and his young wife had come to live in the Providence Plantation or, as the district had begun to be called by that time, the Colony of Rhode Island. He told how they had been forced to leave their comfortable home in England because of persecution there and had come to America believing they would find freedom to worship in their own way in that new land just as the Pilgrims had. But more than fifty years had passed since the Pilgrims came and in that time the Puritan Church had established itself as the religious power of New England. All too soon the young couple had discovered that Puritan church leaders had little more tolerance for views other than their own than did church dignitaries in England.

"We knew persecution in the Bay Colony much as we had at home," he told her. "But at length we heard of the new colony a young Puritan minister named Roger Williams had founded, where folk of all faiths were welcome. He had been banished from the Bay Colony because he could not see eye to eye with the Puritan zealots. When he reached this place of sanctuary he felt it a gift from Heaven and so named the first settlement he made Providence. From that came the Providence Plantation in which the first law is that all who come into it shall enjoy what Master Williams calls 'soul freedom.' So like great numbers of Friends we migrated here," he ended, "and, as thee well knows, we have found here what we came to America to seek and feared we were ne'er to find. So hold this place as sacred ground, my child. For from it the greatest thing for all the world shall grow—the right for a man to own his own soul."

So Hannah had grown up regarding their hilltop and its surrounding hills as sacred. As she became older, however, it grew doubly dear to her because it provided the site for the house of the traveler's candle. She knew her father had selected the location with the greatest care. Most of the Quaker refugees had gone down Narragansett Bay to Aquidneck Island to settle where they could have good homes, opportunities of many kinds, and a life surrounded with their own people. Joshua had settled on a lonely, isolated hilltop because there his house could best provide shelter to the wayfarers making the difficult journey into the new colony. In the years it had stood there hundreds of people of every faith and kind and creed had found rest and refreshment beneath its kindly rooftree. Never in all the years had there been a night when it had not shed its blessed beacon of hospitality upon the trail.

Hannah did not really think all these things as she stood on the doorstep gazing lovingly about at the September landscape—not consciously. Yet they were all there in the landscape and she felt them. For the little house on its wind-swept hilltop with its guardian circle of majestic hills had become a symbol to her of all the things she had come to hold most dear. When she stood looking about, as she did now, the noble calm of those eternal hills filled her anew with a serene and potent faith in the sacred dignity of the human spirit.

As she ran down through the garden between the rows of drying pole beans and yellowing cornstalks and out through the orchard to where the trail into the woods her mother had spoken of as the "river path" began, she felt so borne up by that power her feet hardly seemed to touch the ground.

The river path was not a real trail but just a little footpath Jonathan's small feet had worn through the woods as a short-cut to the spot on the banks of the river where he went to fish. Hannah was all too familiar with it for almost every day she was forced to go there at some time to call her brother home from his fishing. She cupped her hands about her mouth and raised her voice in a well-practiced hail.

An answer came back almost at once from a point not far distant on the trail and in a moment a boyish figure came into sight weaving in and out among the trees at a rapid jog trot. The lad did not wait to reach his sister to give an account of himself but began a shouted explanation as soon as he was within earshot.

"I know what thee wants, Hannah," he panted. " 'Tis the wood-box again. I was on my way back before thee called." Then as he reached her and came to a halt he went on earnestly, "I'd no intent to neglect the wood. Honest, Hannah, I thought to be back within the hour. But the fish were biting too good. Look!" And with a triumphant gesture he held up a fine string of fish threaded through the gills onto a forked stick.

He was a sturdy lad with the same look of comfortable substantialness as his mother. His merry brown eyes looked out of a crop of freckles that almost entirely covered his face, and a shock of hair, sunburned to a dingy straw-color, stood wildly on end above them.

Hannah concealed the gratification she felt at sight of the fish and assumed as good an imitation of her mother's sternest manner as she could muster. "Thee should have filled the box ere thee went, brother. Come quickly now, for the last log is burning."

The boy gave a startled exclamation and, thrusting the string of fish into his sister's hand without a word, bolted off across the orchard.

By the time Hannah reached the lean-to woodshed she found him starting into the house, his arms piled so high with wood his chin rested on the topmost log.

He paused to give her a knowing grin. "So be I get in with wood aplenty while there's still a log burning, Mother won't feel it her bounden duty to scold," he explained.

And he was right. For when Mistress Mapes was confronted with such evidence of the boy's good intentions she contented herself with remarking in a tone supposed to convey dark hints of dire consequences but barely averted, "Well, young man, thee got here just in the nick o' time."

Jonathan made no reply until he had placed a log on the fire and filled the wood-box, then answered with an air of injured virtue, "I'd have been back long ere this, Mother, but that I stayed long enough to catch fish sufficient for the traveler's share as well as ourselves."

Hannah and her father exchanged amused glances. The boy was playing on his mother's special weakness. Most people who set out the traveler's candle contented themselves with sharing their hearth with the wayfarer. Mistress Mapes insisted their hospitality should include a tempting and substantial repast as well. Each evening when she prepared the food for her family she cooked enough for another person, put it in the Dutch oven, and placed the pot upon the hearth amid the ashes so the food would keep warm.

More than half the time it was wasted—for travelers upon their trail were far from an everyday occurrence. In the winter especially, sometimes weeks would go by without their having a single visitor. As a rule travelers took the road again so early in the morning that they were not seen by their hosts. When Mistress Mapes came into the kitchen, the first thing she did was to look into the Dutch oven, and if she found it empty her face would beam with satisfaction. "Look," she would say, " 'twas some poor soul half starved. I venture he was grateful for that good hot food."

Jonathan's contribution of such fine fare for the traveler's pot made complete amends for his neglect of the wood-box. His mother's face was beaming as she took the fish from Hannah and held them up for Joshua to see.

"Look, husband," she said happily, "thee can have thy fill of fish this evening and still leave a fine meal for the traveler."

Joshua put his work aside and came to inspect the catch. Then he and Jonathan set to work cleaning the fish for cooking while Mistress Mapes stirred up a batch of journey cakes and set them on the hearth to bake and Hannah got out the board trestles, laid the trestle-board upon them, and set their wooden trenchers and drinking noggins about.

Before the meal was ready, the rain Joshua had predicted had begun. It started quietly, pattering gently on the thatch at first; but, by the time the meal was over, it had increased to a downpour.

Each night Mistress Mapes laid out a blanket on the settle for the use of their possible guest. Tonight she got out one of Joshua's work frocks as well, remarking as she placed it by the blanket, "Anyone out this night will be drenched to the skin and need a garment to put on while he dries his clothes by the fire." Then turning to Jonathan she added, "Fetch one of the board trestles to stand on the hearth so he'll have a place to hang his wet things."

In like manner, trying to anticipate each need, they had prepared for the coming of a traveler all through the years. Expectation of a guest and, when one did come, speculation about him constituted the drama of their quiet lives. Of a morning when they found that someone had slept beside their fire the whole family would flock eagerly about to see if there were any signs by which they could deduce the nature of their visitor. For days after, Hannah and Jonathan found endless entertainment devising imaginary tales about him.

Once in a while a traveler would remain until the family arose. Those were red-letter days. It was wonderful to sit at the morning meal with a guest beside the board listening to him tell of the place off there beyond the woods from which he had come and of what he planned to do when he reached the place to which he was going.

But, seen or unseen, the Mapes family regarded all their visitors as friends whose welfare was to be considered as equal with their own.

It had become the custom of the family for Hannah to set out the candle. So when the fire was banked for the night and they were all ready to go to their beds—Joshua and Naomi in a lean-to bed-chamber built against the wall behind the fireplace so the chimney warmed it slightly and Hannah and Jonathan at opposite ends of a loft close up under the rafters across the other end of the cabin—Joshua went to the candle box which hung above the mantel, took out a candle, and handed it to the girl.

It was not an ordinary white tallow candle. It was taller and fatter so it would last the night and of a lovely green color—for it was made of bayberry wax. Bayberry candles burned longer and with a steadier flame than those of tallow. They never guttered or doubled up from heat. In every way they were far superior. But though they were much more trouble to make than tallow candles and brought a higher price from his customers, Joshua reserved a large part of his bayberry stock for use as traveler's candles.

Jonathan went to the fireplace, lighted a spill, and brought it to set the wick alight while Hannah held the candle reverently. When the clear, golden flame flowered on the sturdy green stem the room was filled with a delightful fragrance, tangy and fresh as the salt air blowing over the hills where the bayberries which yielded the wax for the candle had grown.

A pewter candle holder with a tin reflector stood on the deep sill of the little recessed window in solitary state. Hannah fitted the candle carefully into it and, burning

18

there in the little window niche, it looked almost as though it were in a shrine.

The rest of the family stood close in a quiet group. Hannah stepped back among them and Joshua said simply, "Let us ask the blessing of safe journey for all travelers."

They all stood silent with bowed heads in the Quaker manner.

The golden flame of the candle burned steady and still. There was no sound but the faint hissing of the banked back-log and the steady drumming of the rain on the thatch. A living silence seemed to rise from the candle flame and from the still figures wrapped in the deep quiet of communion with the Spirit.

Long after they had gone to their beds that living silence seemed to linger in the room like an invisible presence.

2

A TRAVELER FROM A FAR COUNTRY

HANNAH fell asleep lulled by the sound of rain on the thatch. But a high wind rose in the night and woke her with the noise it made. It came in blasts which made the timbers of the little house squeak and rattle and the shutters strain on their hinges. Then there would be a lull and a moment of ominous silence until the next blast came. During one such lull she was about to drift off to sleep again when she was startled wide awake by the click of the latch and then the creak of the door opening softly.

"A traveler!" she thought, sitting up in bed, her heart beating fast with excitement.

She had never been awake to see a traveler enter their house and had always hoped that sometime she might be. She sat tense, waiting for further sound. It was so long before another came that she had begun to conclude disappointedly that what she had heard must have been a trick of the wind. Then a floor board squeaked and there was the sound of cautious footsteps.

Hannah slipped out of bed and crept softly to the stair hole to peer down into the room below. A figure was moving stealthily toward the fire. Her brows drew together in a puzzled frown. The visitor's back was toward her but there was something unmistakably youthful in the slight form clad only in a tattered shirt and torn breeches hanging loose at the knee. In a moment he paused to look about and she got a glimpse of his face. She caught her breath with surprise. The traveler was just a boy!

"Why," she thought, amazed, "he can be little older than I am myself."

In an instant he moved on to the fireplace and, crouching on the hearth, held out shaking hands to the fire. Presently he caught sight of the pot in the ashes and cautiously raised the lid. The savory odor of the food came clear up to Hannah where she watched. Evidently its temptation was too much for the boy. He ate like a starved creature till the pot was empty. Then he settled back with a sigh and once more looked about him. His eyes fell on the blanket and frock Naomi had laid out. He rose softly and got them, slipped off his wet clothing, drew the frock over his head, and let its long folds fall about him like a woman's night-rail. Then he hung the dripping garments on the trestle, wrapped the blanket about himself, and stretched out on the hearth. In a moment the sound of his breathing told the watching girl he was asleep.

She waited until she was sure she would not waken him when she moved, then crept back to bed. She lay listening for a while to that peaceful sound of heavy slumber, but presently she, too, slipped off to sleep.

She was wakened, as she was every morning, by her mother's brisk tread in the room below. She bounded out of bed and ran to the stair hole to look down. The sleeping lad had not wakened. He was lying on the hearth wrapped in the blanket just as she had seen him last. Mistress Mapes was on her way to the fireplace to stir the fire as she always did the first thing in the morning and was almost upon the figure on the hearth before she noted it. Hannah quite plainly heard her gasp of surprise.

The girl jerked off her night-rail and pulled on her few articles of clothing with frantic haste. As she hurried down the steep stair she saw her mother bending over the sleeping boy. At the sound of Hannah's footfall she turned round with a finger to her lips, and tiptoed over to her.

Her face was soft with motherly feeling. " 'Tis but a lad," she whispered, "sleeping like a babe."

At that moment Joshua appeared in the door of the bedchamber. Naomi signaled him a warning, pointing at their sleeping guest. He crossed to the hearth with the light step habitual to him, and the other two came forward cautiously to join him. They were all bending above the sleeper when Jonathan came clattering down the stair, demanding in a loud voice to be told what they were all looking at.

The boy opened his eyes, stared up into the faces bending over him, looked wildly about, and then struggled to rise.

Joshua pressed him back with a soothing hand. "There, there, lad, rest where thee is. 'Tis plain thee was quite tuckered out and thee is welcome to stay here as long as need be."

Recollection of where he was came into the boy's face. He lay back with a look of relief. "Aye, I remember now. I took shelter from the storm in the house where the candle burned in the window, as a man I met on the trail told me to do. I had meant to be on my way long ere this

22

but I must have been so spent I did not waken."

"And a good thing too," put in Naomi, "for the rain is far from over and thee must not start forth again till it stops."

The young traveler sat up, wrapped in his blanket, and looked from one to the other with an expression of interest. "From your speech I judge you to be Quaker folk," he commented.

"Aye," replied Joshua, smiling down upon him kindly, "we are Friends. Thee may know, perchance, that to such all men are friends and brothers. So thee may feel at ease here."

The boy's lips twisted into an ironic smile which made the young face look strangely bitter. "As to any feeling all men brothers, I'd have doubt," he answered flatly. "But, from what I have heard, I judge Quakers to be more kindly than most."

Joshua made no reply. He, in his turn, was looking at the speaker with interest because his speech had also revealed an important thing about him. Joshua had lived amid educated gentle folk in England and the lad's English betrayed him as such a one. An uncomfortable silence fell on the little group. The boy cast an embarrassed glance at his tattered clothing hanging on the trestle before the fire.

"I took off my clothes to dry," he said at length, "and should like to put them on so be there is a place where I can do so."

"Thee can go into the bed-chamber," Naomi told him quickly, "but these things of thine are not fit to put on till they be washed and mended. My husband will give thee what thee may need. Wrap the blanket about thyself

25

and go now and a hot meal will be ready when thee gets back."

Later when he returned from the bed-chamber dressed in some of Joshua's clothing, clean and neatly combed, his appearance bore out Joshua's conclusions about him. He looked like a young gentleman. He expressed his thanks with simple graciousness, his voice taking a rising inflection when he reached the place where he should have spoken the name of his hosts, implying that he did not know it.

Joshua quickly supplied the lack, asking quite naturally in return, "And what might thy name be, lad?"

A shadow crossed the boy's face. He looked down, seeming to struggle with himself. When he raised his eyes there was pain in them, thinly veiled by an air of assumed unconcern. "I have no name," he answered bluntly. "Call me what you will."

A compassionate tenderness welled up in Joshua's eyes. "Names are of small import," he said gently. "My good wife and I can call thee son, so be thee would not mind our doing so."

The boy's lips trembled and to hide the fact he turned his face quickly aside and stood silent, the muscles of his throat working convulsively.

Naomi saw his state and came quickly to his assistance by announcing that the meal was ready and engaging the attention of all the family by assigning a task to each in getting it on the table. By the time they were ready to sit down the boy had gained command of himself again.

No questions were asked as to whence he had come or whither he was going—for those were matters about which every traveler who came into the Mapes home was left free to volunteer information or not as he saw fit. But when the meal was nearly over, the boy asked how far he was from Providence and, when Joshua had told him, amazed them all by announcing that he was on his way there to see Roger Williams.

"Tales have been told me about him that I found nigh impossible to credit," he added. "I want to meet the man and see whether there be any truth in them."

"I take it thee means tales of his fight to establish a state where all men have the right to think as they will," replied Joshua.

The boy nodded. "Aye. But I do not believe them. Men are not like that."

Hannah had ministered to the guest's needs with shy friendliness during the meal but had taken no part in the conversation. That assertion stung her out of her diffidence and brought a quick, earnest retort. "Some men are," she declared. "I know it for truth, not only because of Master Williams, but because my own father is such a one."

The boy turned to look at her, a flicker of cynical amusement in his eyes. It died away before the clear earnestness of her gaze and a questioning thoughtfulness took its place. His glance wandered speculatively to Joshua. "I believe he might be—so be any could be like that," he said, more as if he were speaking to himself than to the others. Then he turned back to Hannah with a friendly smile in which a gleam of humor twinkled. "He grants others the right to keep their own council, in any case. He has not e'en asked me how I chanced to be in his house last night."

"Why should I ask?" laughed Joshua. "Thee came in

like any traveler who had seen our candle." He gave a little shrug of philosophic acceptance. "A man who leaves his latchstring out to strangers must content himself to let folk tell what they will."

The young visitor did not reply at once but sat looking down at his trencher as though in an effort to come to some conclusion. When he looked up his face was set in lines of pained decision. "Sir," he said, "it had been my intent to tell my tale to no one. Now I know 'twould ease me to tell it to you though 'tis so wild a tale and I am here by a mischance so strange I can scarce expect any to believe it."

Joshua gave him a gravely quiet smile. "We will believe it, lad," he answered simply.

The tense lines of the boy's face relaxed with grateful relief. "Thank you, sir," he replied. He sat silent a moment, crumbling a bit of journey cake as though seeking a way to begin. At length he looked up and asked abruptly, "Have you perchance heard of the unfortunates seamen term 'kids'?"

"Kids," repeated Joshua, bewildered. "Nay, I have ne'er heard the term."

" 'Tis the name they give lads kidnapped in Europe and brought to the colonies to be sold as slaves."

"Slaves!" echoed Hannah, her eyes wide with horror. "Thee means boys are stolen from their homes and sold into bondage? Surely that could ne'er be possible."

"Aye, but it is. There are many ship's captains who make tidy fortunes at the business. Right now Ireland is the most fertile field for their efforts, for the sad land has been so disrupted by England's political upheavals that there are many lads with no families to make search for

28

them." He paused a moment as though nerving himself for a distressing revelation, then added, "My home was there and I am such a one."

Joshua gave an exclamation which was a mixture of dismay, indignation, and sympathy. The others were shocked into silence.

The boy hastened to reassure them. "I was not sold as a slave though. I had the good fortune to escape first—and that is how I come to be here. Our ship was making for Boston, but a storm came up and blew us south of our course. 'Twas so bad our captain ran into Cape Cod Bay for shelter and anchored there till the blow be spent. That night when we captives were brought up on deck for exercise, as we were each night so we might not lose our strength and thus not bring so good a price as slaves, I found we were so close to land I could see lights twinkling on the shore."

"Plymouth, that would be," Joshua put in.

The lad nodded. "Aye, it was. I found out later." He was so intent on his tale the interruption did not divert him and he continued quickly, "I am a strong swimmer and was sure that, were it not for the leg chains we wore, I could swim ashore. The sailor who always brought us on deck hated his captain. I knew that, could he do so in safety to himself, he would be glad enough to have one of his captives escape. So I told him that would he but unlock the gyves about my ankles, I would jump overboard with the chains on and his captain would think I had chosen to drown myself rather than be sold into bondage. He consented to do it."

Jonathan's eyes were big as saucers with excited admiration. "And thee wasn't scared of drowning?" he asked

29

ın a voice hushed with awe.

The other boy shrugged. "Better to drown than be sold as a slave. 'Twas ten to one the heavy fetters would drag me to the bottom ere I could get them off. But there was the one chance I could get free of them in time. I hid on deck when the rest were taken below. As soon as the ship got under way again I jumped."

All the listeners but Jonathan gave involuntary exclamations of horror. He leaned forward, urging breathlessly, "Go on telling. What happened next?"

The story teller cast the lad an indulgent smile. It was not unpleasant to be the object of such interest. "Well, you see," he continued with a wry smile and a shrug, "I am here. I did have trouble getting off the gyves, and by the time I was free of them the chains had dragged me down so far that the ship was but a blur in the darkness when I reached the surface again. I make no doubt all on board, e'en the man who had helped me, thought me lying at the bottom of the bay." He paused, looking steadfastly at Joshua. "That is the reason, sir, I have no name. The lad who bore it is thought to be dead and buried deep in the sea. I shall let him rest there."

"But thy parents, lad," protested Naomi, "and what other kin thee has left in Ireland—they will be broken-hearted grieving for thee! Surely we must let them know thee is safe."

"Better still, we could send thee back to them," added Joshua. "Roger Williams could arrange the matter, I am sure."

The boy's lips set in a stubborn line. "None there will grieve for me—and I have no wish to return. Nay, I'll stay here in the colonies and start a new life."

30

There was such finality in his tone the chandler could only agree. "Well, lad, thee is thy own master and none can gainsay thee." He gave a wry smile as if at some recollection of his own. "Thee will not be the first to start a new life here under desperate odds. But thee will need a name e'en for life here in the wilderness."

"Then perchance you will give me one," suggested the boy, "since really I am entering on my new life here in your house."

The family seized on the idea with enthusiasm and one after another suggested names. But Joshua would have none of them.

"Those are all names for Quaker folk," he laughed. "They'd fit but ill on an Irish lad." He thought a moment. "What about Patrick? That is a name all Irish honor because of their great saint."

The boy greeted the suggestion with a dry laugh. " 'Twould have no honor with me on that score—for I pay no respect to saints, Irish or otherwise. But I'd be glad to bear the name of Patrick in memory of an Irish lad I played with as a boy and dearly loved." He glanced about the circle and added, "I myself am not Irish."

"Not Irish," repeated Joshua, confused. "But I thought thee said thee came from there."

"And so I did. I was born there also; but my parents were English Puritans. They were among those sent into Ireland by Cromwell during the Commonwealth. My father was a man of substance and a power in the Puritan party and was made a sort of over-lord there. He was a stern and rigid Roundhead and, while the Commonwealth lasted, ruled the Irish with an iron hand. But when the Commonwealth fell and a Church of England king was on the throne again, Puritans in Ireland were in no better case than the Catholic Irish themselves. 'Twas a fine welter of religious strife you can well believe. And 'twas into that I was born. I have ne'er known aught else. Do you wonder I have scant love for saints?"

The chandler let an eloquent glance answer that question, then inquired with interest if the boy's parents were still in Ireland.

A curtain of bitter reserve seemed to fall about the boy. He did not respond at once but sat in a kind of stony silence as though making up his mind to refuse to reply altogether. When he did answer it was in a voice restrained to cool aloofness. "I suppose so. I had not heard from them for many months ere I was kidnapped. I was working on the docks in Belfast at the time." He paused an instant, then continued in a coldly level tone, "I had left my father's house for good and all."

The Mapes family stared at him in shocked silence. With them family love was such a deep and living bond that it seemed unthinkable a boy should voluntarily cut himself off from his home. No one spoke for so long the pause was growing painful. So, at length, Joshua cleared his throat and remarked doubtfully, "Beyond doubt thee had thy own reasons for taking so dire a step."

"They seemed reasons to me." The boy's voice was sharp with an urgent need to break down that wall of disapproving silence. "In my father's house only one set of people could be thought right or good. All others were considered spawn of the devil."

Joshua and Naomi exchanged a quick, understanding glance. They had been considered spawn of the devil by the Puritans themselves. They knew how cruelly unrelenting that attitude could be. It was a dreadful thing for a boy to quit his father's house, of course; but the fact that he had done so for such a reason made their hearts go out to him with especial warmth.

Naomi's voice had a new tone as she said gently, "Well, lad, that is all behind thee now. Here thee will see naught of it."

The remark brought a skeptical smile to the boy's lips. "I've no expectation of the like," he answered bluntly. "But at least I'll have a chance to hear what ideas your Roger Williams has for trying to make it so."

Joshua gave a laugh of pleased recognition. "As I live, lad, thy kidnappers did thee a real service. They brought thee right to the place where thee could meet Master Williams as thee so much desired."

"Then they did it unbeknown to me," replied the boy, "for I had not heard of him till I got ashore near Plymouth. A fisherman who found me on the beach more dead than alive and befriended me told me about him. He said strangers were no longer welcome in the Plymouth colony and advised me to push on to Providence where he said all who came were gladly taken in. He told me also how to make the journey and that on the way I could find shelter wherever I saw a candle burning in a window by night."

The mention of the traveler's candle brought a flash of quick interest into Hannah's face. "And did thee see many?" she asked eagerly.

"Not till I got to the outlying settlements of the Plymouth territory. Then I saw several. But I did not go into any of the houses. I would not have come into your house either but for the urging of the man I met on the trail and that I was so driven by the storm."

"But why should thee hesitate to go in where the candle bade thee welcome?" insisted the girl.

The boy gave an apologetic little laugh. "I could not bring myself to go into the house of a stranger like that. I could not believe any folk could be so trustful as really to want a passerby to come into their homes in the dead of night. Back in my own home no one would. They'd think to be murdered in their beds."

Joshua chuckled. "Many here have the same notion," he admitted. Then his face became suddenly intent with deep conviction. "But not those who set out the traveler's candle. They have learned the power of trust." His voice was vibrant with feeling and his eyes glowed as though they too had candles lighted in them. "The traveler's candle is a token of a man's faith in his fellow-man. And that no man will violate."

A reluctant admiration came into the boy's eyes. "I wish I had your sureness of it, Master Mapes," he said, and there was wistfulness in his tone. "But this I'm bound to say. I owe you and yours thanks for much more than food and shelter. For I have seen things in your house I did not know were to be found anywhere. It has put heart into me for trying to find some foothold here in your colony."

The chandler waved away the thanks and laid hold of the boy's last words. "That brings me to the very thing I had in mind to ask thee. Has thee any plan for how thee will go about finding placement here, lad?"

"In a way. I thought I would seek out some honest tradesman who might have need of a helper and apprentice myself to him. In that way I could earn my bread and at the same time learn a trade."

Joshua's eyes went to his wife's face in swift question. Naomi's answering look gave prompt reply. Then the two glances merged in warm agreement.

Naomi nodded a thoughtful approval. "That seems a good idea," she commented. "Many a lad has got a good start in life that way. Did thee have any special trade in mind, son?" Her voice sounded as though she might be speaking to a son of her very own.

The boy shook his head. "Unfortunately I know naught of trades." He gave a little laugh of scorn at himself. "I was reared to be a Puritan gentleman."

"Well," said Joshua slowly, as though thinking of the idea for the first time, "what would thee say to the trade of candle chandler? I stand in need of a helper right now."

A pained flush flooded the boy's pale cheeks. "I must not let myself think of it at all—grateful as I am for the suggestion. For I know you only make it to help me."

"But thee is wrong, son," Naomi assured him hastily. "My husband does badly need a helper. Hannah and I know that all too well, since it is we who must help him all the time."

The chandler's face expressed emphatic agreement. "That's naught but the truth, boy. I give thee my word. The busy season is just upon us and during that time I could use two helpers, let alone one. And, did I have a helper the year round, I could expand my trade as much again."

Dawning hope and distressed indecision mingled in the boy's expression. "But I'd really be no help to you, sir," he protested, "for I know naught of chandlering and you would only have to take your time to teach me."

Hannah was leaning forward, her elbows on the table,

her face glowing with eagerness. "Thee could learn easily. Candle making is really an easy trade. Even I, a simple girl, know most of it. I could teach thee nearly everything and Father would not have any bother with thee at all." She paused hopefully, waiting for the boy to give his answer. Then, as he made none, she went on earnestly, "Please, Patrick, do stay with us. We need thee—really we do."

The boy's tense jaw relaxed. The sharp lines of his face softened. Hearing his new name spoken for the first time with such eager unconsciousness disarmed him utterly. His eyes traveled questioningly from face to face. It was impossible to doubt the sincerity in all of them. Maybe they did need him. At least they seemed to want him. He turned back to Joshua, and when he spoke his voice was husky. "Very well, Master Mapes. I'll stay with you—and do the best I can to be a help."

3

PATRICK STARTS LIFE AS A CHANDLER

I T was the second day after Patrick had so unexpectedly become a member of the chandler's family. The rain was over. Mellow September sunshine poured in at the open door, making a long oblong of gold on the puncheon floor. Puffs of soft air, laden with the fragrance of wet earth and a mixture of tangy autumn smells, blew in at the open window holes.

Patrick and Hannah sat at the big work table. Three great spools of wicking and a pile of completed wick on the table between them gave evidence that Hannah was giving the new apprentice his first lesson in the tasks of the candle chandler.

"We make both kinds of candles," she was saying, twisting wick with the air of an expert, "the molded sort and dips. But the wick is the same for both." Her tone was that of a young schoolmistress and her face wore the sober expression of one who imparts important knowledge.

Patrick sat stiff with attention, his eyes riveted upon her with troubled concern lest he miss one detail of the instruction in the trade on which he was embarking. He was wearing his own clothing again, now washed and neatly mended. His face had lost a little of its starved and haggard look, but there was still a weary droop in the thin shoulders.

Joshua was perched in his accustomed place before his work-bench; but Naomi had abandoned the wick making and sat by the open door, deep in the task of making over some of Joshua's clothing into garments for Patrick. She had gathered the boy into her family circle with whole-hearted enthusiasm so now, as she sat busily stitching, her face glowed with the look of rapt contentment it always wore when she was engaged in a labor of love.

Hannah laid aside her finished wick and, drawing off an end of wicking from one of the spools, began looping the unwinding strand about two wooden pegs set in the table. "We measure off enough wick for a dozen candles at one time this way," she said, smiling across at her pupil. "Thee may note the pegs are some eight inches apart. That is the length of a common candle. Each one takes twice that length of wick since the strand must be doubled. Then the two halves are twisted together, both in order to make it firmer and so there may be a loop at the top by which it may be hung in the mold or on a rod for dipping."

While she was speaking she went on looping so dexterously that the pegs were filled with wicking when she finished. She slipped it off and cut through the loop at one end with a great shears that lay beside her. "There," she announced; "that batch of wick is ready for twisting." Then she pushed the spool across to Patrick. "Do thee try looping some thyself now."

But as he reached to take it she seemed to have another thought. "Nay," she said, "wait a bit. First thee should know the different wick we use. This is our common kind. The other spools are different. Compare them and see can thee see in what way."

Patrick drew the three spools to him and, unwinding a bit from each, examined the strands side by side. "Aye, I see they are," he agreed.

The one from the spool Hannah had been using was a twisted strand, almost tan in color and harsh to the touch. The second was made up of a number of yarn-like threads, not twisted but laid side by side. It was pure white in color, flexible and soft. The third brought an exclamation of delight from the boy. It was silvery white with little brown flecks here and there and glistened with the sheen of silk. As it slipped through his fingers it was as smooth and soft as a baby's hair.

"What in the world is it?" he questioned, marveling.

The girl's eyes shone with pleasure. "I'll tell thee of that one last," she replied "—for 'tis the best. This first, the common sort, we spin ourselves. 'Tis made from hemp we get from near-by farmers in trade for candles. That is why 'tis so harsh and dark in color. The second is made from cotton and is woven on great machines in England. We have to buy it from a chandler shop in Newport because as yet there is no cotton grown here. We do not use much of it for 'tis costly compared to what we spin ourselves. But some customers insist upon it." She paused to give him one of her beaming smiles. "And now the third. I venture thee could ne'er guess from what that is made."

Patrick admitted he could not.

"From the down of plants," she replied. " 'Tis thistledown mostly—though there is down from milkweed and other plants in it as well."

"Thistledown," echoed the boy in a wondering tone. "But how can stuff so fragile be fashioned into such a strand?"

39

"We spin it," replied Hannah. " 'Tis really little less trouble to handle than wool fleece. The gathering is the difficult part. We know all the plants that seed themselves thus, just where they grow and when they ripen. A body must get to them ere the seeds loosen and the wind blows the down away. We gather all we can. But it is ne'er a sufficient store." Her eyes brightened with pleasure, remembering it. "A lot together is a lovely sight to see. Would thee like to see some? We pack it away in tight-covered baskets till we can spin it."

Patrick said he would love to, so she jumped up, ran to the cupboard in the corner, and brought back a covered wicker hamper.

"Open it carefully," she cautioned. "A puff of air would have the down all about the room."

Patrick raised the lid just enough to peep in at the fluffy, silken mass, then cautiously reaching in with finger and thumb drew out a few of the fairy-like tufts attached to tiny brown seeds. He closed the basket softly and, placing them on his other palm, sat looking at the delicate, silvery seed carriers. A pensive far-away expression came into his eyes and presently he said musingly, "I used to gather them too, when I was a little chap at school in England. We used to play a game with them. We'd blow one off our hands and say:

" 'Thistledown, thistledown, blow away,
Show me the land where I shall stay.'
Then we'd watch where the wind took them ana from the direction they went we'd make guesses as to where we were to live." He gave a strange little laugh. "I remember now mine would always sail off to the west. Perchance, e'en then 'twas my fate to come to America."

He held out his hand and blew gently on the down. It rose into the sunlit air, sailed about a moment—then settled to the floor.

Hannah gave a little gasp, the eyes of the two young people met, and they stood looking at each other in silence.

"Does it mean thee was intended to come here to stay?" the girl asked at length in a hushed tone.

Patrick shrugged. "So be it has a meaning at all, it might. 'Tis naught but a childish game, you know."

His eyes rested a moment longer on the girl's quiet face; then his gaze wandered around the crude cabin, resting on Joshua's slight figure bending above his work in tranquil industry, then on Naomi stitching busily with that strange look of a contentment so beyond the bounds of ordinary human satisfaction on her face. Finally his eyes came back to Hannah's face again. And there was a faint reflection of the peace of the others in them. "It might be well for me an it did," he added quietly.

When Hannah had returned the basket to the cupboard and resumed her place at the table, she did not take up her work at once but sat gazing at the boy with something like reverent awe. "Thee has been to school in England," she said at length. "What a sight of wonderful things thee must know."

He replied with a dry laugh, "Little of that is like to be of much use to me here. 'Twould be more useful had I learned to spin."

The remark was intended as an ironic jest. Hannah took it with utter seriousness. "Thee can learn with little trouble," she told him gravely. " 'Tis not so difficult."

The boy stared at her in blank amazement. "You mean I should—really?"

41

"To be sure," she replied in a matter-of-fact tone. "Spinning wick takes more time than all the rest of making candles. Father spins wick when Mother and I are too busy with household tasks to do it and he has no other work on hand. Jonathan has learned of late also and can now ply the wheel right deftly and turn out a fairly sightly strand."

The mental picture of the freckled, shock-headed Jonathan sitting tamely in the chimney corner spinning like a maiden was too much for Patrick. He burst into a peal of hearty laughter.

Mistress Mapes looked up from her sewing with a happy smile. "Now that's what I like to hear," she exclaimed. "There's naught so good as laughter in the house."

Joshua turned round to add a comment of his own. "Aye, laughter is oil for the wheels of the home. What was it struck thy funny bone, lad?"

Patrick told him and ended doubtfully, "But plainly 'tis funny only to me. Hannah seemed to see naught to laugh at in it."

"Hannah is too used to the like. She has known naught else all her life but to see boys set to spinning the same as their sisters. In a new, wild land each pair of hands must do whate'er they can do." He gave his mild, whimsical smile. "Thee will see many things here that will seem strange to thee—but thee will get used to them."

Patrick did not reply at once. For a moment he felt the traditions of his old life rising up in resistance to the crude pattern of this strange new world. Then suddenly, across that feeling cut the sharp remembrance of other things in the old world—the unending conflict of wills and the merciless intolerance he had hated so bitterly, the tyranni-

42

cal cruelties which had clouded his youth.

A reminiscent shadow blotted out the signs of his recent laughter. He sat in brooding silence a moment longer, then answered with quiet positiveness, "Naught could be so hard to get used to as what I have left behind, sir."

Joshua did not need to be told what those things were. He knew them all too well—and from a much more personal experience than Patrick's. But he was a man grown and the path he had taken was of his own choosing. That knowledge of them should have been visited on a child filled his kind heart with rebellion, and with an intense desire to blot out those unhappy memories and give the boy a clean slate to start with here in the New World. The new work the boy was undertaking would be a start, he thought. So now he deliberately turned his mind back to it.

"How are the wicks coming?" he asked, and then without waiting for an answer continued, "Hannah and thee will have to make all haste getting a quantity ready today, for we'll have our hands full preparing the bayberry wax to start making the dips as soon as the berries are gathered. And it looks now as though that would be on the morrow. For since it has cleared so fair, seems like we can have the bayberry bee then as we planned."

Patrick looked puzzled. "Bayberry bee," he repeated. "What is that, sir?"

The chandler's eyes flew wide with surprise. "Mercy on us, lad! Has thee ne'er heard of bees?"

The boy admitted with a flush that he never had.

Mistress Mapes dropped her work in consternation. "Were there no bees in thy home, boy? How in the world did folk get their work done?"

Hannah came to his rescue. "A bee is a kind of party.

43

Only at a bee there is some big task all must work at together so a lot of work gets done in a hurry. A bayberry
bee is a party for picking the bayberries. 'Tis great fun.
All the folk of the neighborhood meet at some place agreed
upon, each family bringing a fine lot of food for a common meal. When the picking is done the meal is spread,
and when it is finished there are games and races and all
manner of jests."

"Most of our good neighbor folk will be at the bee on
the morrow," added Joshua, "so 'twill be a fine chance for
thee to meet them all."

That reminded Mistress Mapes the lad would need the
clothes she was fixing for him, and she resumed her sewing with redoubled vigor. Joshua turned to his bench and
Hannah went back to her instruction in wick preparation.

It was not long until Patrick had mastered the art of
measuring, cutting, and twisting wick and was working
with deft rapidity. A busy quiet fell upon the room and
for a time the boy was conscious only of its tranquillity.
But, at length, an insistent sound began to force itself on
his attention. At first he thought it must be a woodpecker
off in the woods, for it was certainly the sound made by
something tapping on wood. Presently, however, he abandoned the idea. No woodpecker could produce a sound so
sustained and so evenly timed.

"Tap, tap," it went. "Tap—tap, tap." There was a brief
pause then again, "Tap, tap—tap, tap—tap."

He could contain his curiosity no longer. "Listen, Hannah," he said, "can you hear that queer noise?"

Hannah paused in her work, listened a moment, and
answered casually, "Oh, that. 'Tis Jonathan pounding
meal."

Their talk had drawn Mistress Mapes' attention to the sound and she too paused, needle suspended. "Hark a moment," she commanded. The rhythmically spaced tapping went persistently on. "Pounding meal!" she ejaculated at length with fine scorn. "I wish he were! Hannah, run out and tell that doless brother of thine to have done chattering with Hiram Tufts across the hill and get at our meal at once."

Patrick was completely mystified.

Hannah noticed his bewildered look and asked laughingly as she rose, "Would thee like to come out with me and see for thyself?"

It was exactly what he wanted to do. He had not been outside to look around since the storm had cleared and had been eager for the chance.

The day before the rain-soaked hilltop encircled with darkly brooding hills had seemed a dreary and desolate spot. Today, with the sky an intense, shining blue across which a rollicking breeze was sending masses of little, puffy white clouds racing and tumbling like playful sheep in a meadow, and with the trees on the hills waving and nodding as though in friendly greeting, it seemed quite a different place. Crossing the garden he felt his spirits rising and by the time he reached the barnyard he was ready to enjoy whatever it was they had come to see. The tapping had been growing louder as they neared the barn and when they rounded its corner they saw what was causing it.

Jonathan stood beside a waist-high stump the top of which had been rounded out into a basin. Above it a stout length of wood, rounded at the end and shaped so it could be grasped conveniently, was suspended by a thong to the top of a near-by sapling. The elastic young tree had been

45

bent over and secured firmly in a sturdy forked pole so that its tip was held just over the hollowed cavity and the length of wood hung about a foot above it.

Patrick saw at a glance what Hannah could have meant by saying Jonathan was pounding meal. The basin hollowed out in the stump would make a splendid mortar and the rounded length of wood a pestle which could be operated with a minimum of effort because the sapling supported its weight and lifted it with its natural rebound after each downward pull.

But evidently—as Mistress Mapes had intimated—Jonathan was not using it for any such useful purpose. There was no grain in the basin and the boy's carefully timed strokes seemed to be solely for the purpose of creating the tapping sound. He was so intent on accomplishing this according to some special design of his own that he did not notice their approach until they stood beside him. When he caught sight of his sister, he stopped abruptly and stooped hastily to pick up a gourd dipper lying on the lid of a closely woven wicker basket standing beside the stump.

"I was just going to start the meal—really I was, Hannah," he assured the girl, raising the basket lid and dipping up a gourdful of corn.

Hannah gave him a glance of eloquent skepticism. The boy was about to pour the corn into the mortar but she stopped him, saying, "Since thee has dallied this long, thee can waste a few more minutes to talk to Hiram and show Patrick how thee uses the mill for it." Then she turned to Patrick to explain. "The Tufts live the other side of the hill. 'Tis a hard journey there and back, so the boys worked out this way of talking to each other."

46

"We made up a language," Jonathan volunteered proudly. "A special number of taps together mean one word and another number some other. We can say lots of things."

"Say something now then," suggested Patrick.

Hannah's eyes were mischievous. "Aye, tell Hiram thee must stop chattering and get at pounding our meal."

The boy wrinkled his freckled nose at his sister, then started tapping. After a few moments he paused with the pestle suspended, listening intently. A fairy-like echo came faintly from over the hilltop.

"What did Hiram say?" asked Hannah when it ended.

Jonathan gave a sheepish grin. "He said 'twas the same with him," he replied, picked up the dipper again, emptied the corn into the mortar, and started pounding in good earnest.

Patrick watched fascinated, as the kernels were rapidly reduced to a fine powder. There was a hole in the stump below the basin, stopped with a wooden plug. Just beneath it a round box made of birch bark stood on the ground at the foot of the stump. When there was no more whole corn left in the mortar, Jonathan pulled out the plug and a stream of meal flowed into the box.

The visitor was filled with a desire to try his hand at using the pestle himself. "May I do the next lot?" he begged. Then, as he took Jonathan's place and started pounding, he exclaimed with enthusiasm, "Why, 'tis near no work at all, the way the pestle is hung."

"Pestle," Jonathan repeated with questioning interest. "Is that the name for it in thy home? Here we call it a mortar sweep and the whole thing a sweep and mortar mill."

47

"To be sure," said Patrick in a tone of pleased recognition. "The sapling works the same as a well sweep. I have seen many wells of the kind in Ireland." That seemed to make him think of something. He paused in his pounding and looked curiously about. "Where is your well, by the way? I just thought, I've not seen it yet."

Jonathan glowed with pride. "We don't have one. We don't have to. We've got an ever-flowing barrel."

Hannah's eyes were twinkling with mischief. "Thee was sitting on it yesterday."

The boy flushed. He had mistaken a thing that turned out to be a barrel covered with a hinged lid for a stool the day before, and had only discovered his error when Naomi had been forced to ask him to get up so she could dip water from it. "Oh, that," he said, "I thought 'twas but a rain barrel."

" 'Tis ever-flowing," insisted Jonathan in the tone of one whose most treasured possession has been belittled.

Patrick looked helplessly at Hannah.

"Come in and I'll show thee," she told him.

He relinquished the pestle to Jonathan and they hastened back to the house. She led him to the corner where the upper part of a barrel stood up above the floor at just the right height to be mistaken for a stool.

"Look way down to the bottom of the barrel," she told him when she had raised the lid, "and thee can see the water flowing in. 'Tis piped down from a living spring up on the hill in poplar pump-logs. And see that little hole at the top of the water at the other side. That is the run-off. When the barrel is full the water runs out there and is carried down through a hollowed sumac pipe to be used to make a spring cellar. It is there we store our fats for the candle making. The cold spring water keeps the cellar cool enough that they keep sweet there all summer. I will show thee."

She raised a trap-door in the floor beside the barrel and a draft of cool, damp air blew up into their faces. A flight of rough steps led downward and the girl went before him to their bottom.

The boy found himself standing in a rock-walled room through which the overflow from the barrel made a little stream flowing in a shallow bed hewn in the rock. Shelves for butter and milk and all other foods which needed to be kept in a cool place lined one wall, and against the other stood the row of casks that held the candle fats. The air was so cool that in a few moments the boy felt chilled and was glad to turn back to the steps which would take him to the warmer world above.

Hannah went before him up the steps and his head had just emerged from the trap-door when Jonathan burst in, calling excitedly, "Come quick, everybody. There's a stranger comin' horseback. He just rode over the hill."

Mistress Mapes rose hastily, letting her sewing fall unnoticed to the floor. "Horseback!" she repeated incredulously, starting for the door. "Whoever could that be?"

Patrick's heart gave a terrified leap into his throat and he stopped short on the stair. Ever since his escape from the slave ship he had steadfastly shut his mind against the thought of pursuit and recapture. Now it leapt out at him. After all, the captain might not have thought him dead. The man who had helped him might have told. This might be someone come to drag him back into slavery. He had an overpowering impulse to bolt back into the cellar and pull the door down upon himself.

49

But Hannah was waiting impatiently for him to reach the top so she could close the trap and follow her mother. So, in spite of the dread that gripped him, he forced his dragging feet on up the stairs. When he had almost reached the top, Joshua passed on his way to join Naomi. He glanced at the boy and, as though discerning what was passing in his mind, flashed him a humorous glance of reassurance. It was almost as if he had winked.

Patrick stood staring after the slight figure in startled surprise. That look had given him a glimpse of a Joshua he had not seen before. He had been so moved by the chandler's gentle kindness and benevolent understanding that those were the characteristics he had felt in him. But that look, which made fright something to be laughed away, and a courageous assurance he saw now in that slim back revealed a different aspect of his character.

Stories he had heard of the fearlessness of Quakers flashed through his mind—stories of how some of their leaders had refused to doff their hats in the presence of the king, of how many of them braved the lash and even death with such calm and cheerfulness that the sureness of their persecutors was shaken.

Joshua was like that—he saw that now. He was really afraid of nothing. He would face any danger undaunted when doing so for what he thought was right. That look, so like a wink, had been his way of assuring a frightened boy he need have no fear—for the Quaker knew himself to be more than a match for any such mean creature as the captain of a slave ship.

Patrick's heart resumed its normal beat. He knew he was safe in the chandler's house. More important still, some measure of that dauntless fearlessness had been imparted to him. His mind swung back to consciousness of where he was and he recalled that Hannah was waiting for him, holding the trap-door.

He cast her an apologetic smile. "I'm sorry, Hannah," he said quietly. "I was looking at your father—thinking something about him."

Then, with an unfaltering step and high-held head, he came up the remaining steps, took the door from her hand, and closed it firmly.

4

RED NEIGHBORS

THE Mapes family stood on the doorstep awaiting their visitor. Patrick had lingered just within the door, thinking it discreet to remain out of sight until the identity of the stranger could be determined. But when the horseman was near enough to be recognized, Joshua set his fears at rest.

"What does thee mean, son, getting us all excited?" he remarked to Jonathan, giving the boy's ear a playful tweak. "That is no stranger. 'Tis Master Jenks from the new iron mills down at the Falls."

"Well, how was I to know?" the lad replied in a crestfallen tone. "I'd ne'er seen the man ere this."

Patrick gave a sigh of relief and slipped out to join the group. Hannah felt him behind her and moved over without speaking, to give him place between herself and her father.

The rider drew rein in front of them just then and Joshua greeted him with cordial friendliness. " 'Tis good to see thee at our doorstep, neighbor. Light down and let my boy here take thy horse."

The visitor shook his head. "Nay, I can tarry but a moment. There are a score of neighbors I must get to as soon as may be." He glanced about the circle impressively. "I'm

52

riding round giving warning."

"Warning," repeated Joshua with a questioning smile. "Of what?"

"Of danger," replied Master Jenks, making his voice sound ominous. "Redskins have been sighted in the vicinity."

Patrick felt a chill run up his spine and tingle in the roots of his hair. He had read tales of the American Indians and their horrible ways. He stole cautious glances about to see how the others were taking this terrifying news. To his amazement none of them showed any signs of alarm. Joshua looked as though he were trying to suppress a smile. The faces of the rest of the family expressed nothing but courteous attention. When the Quaker spoke, his tone was one of polite appreciation of a friendly service.

"We give thee thanks for coming to warn us, friend," he said warmly. Then his smile twinkled forth a little and he continued in a deprecating voice, "But I scarce think we need take alarm from seeing a few Indians about. We look to see families of them passing this time of year, for 'tis the season when they go back to their winter wigwams in sheltered places in the hills after spending most of the summer camping beside the rivers or the bay where they can live with ease for several months on fish and other sea foods." He paused and added apologetically, "Thee is more or less a newcomer in these parts and not as familiar with their ways as we."

Master Jenks waved the last comment aside. "The lot that has been sighted could scarce be a family. 'Tis a goodly band. They are camped down by the falls. Till they move on none of our folk must leave their homes.

And by no means must they go out on the hills on the morrow to pick bayberries as was planned."

The edict against the bayberry bee brought an exclamation of violent protest from Jonathan. Joshua placed a quick, restraining hand on his shoulder and the boy fell silent, glowering wrathfully.

"Do they not move on within a day or so," the visitor continued, "we'd best take steps to convert the mill into a defensible house where all can take shelter in case of need."

Joshua raised his brows in mild disagreement. "I doubt that will prove needful. Our tribes have e'er been peaceable. Elsewhere the natives have caused trouble, but we who live here in the territory of the Narragansetts and the Pokanokets stand in rare good fortune. The Narragansetts are held to their oldtime peace pledges by their friendship with Roger Williams. The Pokanokets remember the love their sachem, Massasoit, bore the first Pilgrim settlers and forbear to break the treaty of peace kept for fifty years."

The other man looked unconvinced. "As to the Narragansetts I've no knowledge. I only hope they're as loving as Master Williams thinks they are. But back in the Bay Colony where I hail from folk have long since lost faith in the friendship of the Pokanokets. Massasoit's eldest son, Alexander, hadn't been sachem two years after his father's death when he was suspected of plotting against us. And there's not been a year since, either in his reign or in that of his brother, Philip, who came after him, but that there's been some rumor of devilment afoot."

"Aye, rumors," echoed Joshua. "Naught was proved against Wamsutta—or Alexander as thee calls him—either during his life or after his untimely death for which his

54

family held the English responsible. Nor against Metacom, either, in the near ten years he has been sachem."

Master Jenks cocked his head inquiringly. "Metacom," he repeated. "You mean Philip, the present sachem?"

The chandler gave a smile of mingled assent and apology. "I like better to call our Indian friends by the names of their own race. English names seem to fit as ill upon them as do English ways."

"They take to 'em fast enough," retorted the other.

" 'Twas Massasoit who gave his sons the English names. He did so out of the love he bore the white men. But 'twas a grievous error. When Sachem Metacom—or Metacomet, as his tribesmen say the name—terms himself King Philip, it makes him look a simple creature strutting in borrowed grandeur. And 'tis a pity, for in truth he is a ruler of parts and a proud monarch in his own right."

Master Jenks' eyes narrowed with sharp questioning. "You know him then—this Metacom, since that is the way you like to style him?"

"I could scarce say I know him," Joshua replied in the modest tone of one who disclaims acquaintance with royalty, "but I have had speech with him at times when I have had occasion to visit him with Roger Williams on matters of business related to the boundary lines of the land purchased for the Plantation from his father."

Patrick looked from one man to the other in puzzled amazement. This intimate discussion of Indian personalities was most confusing. From what he had read he had pictured Indians as utter savages—creatures so completely removed from the white man's way of life that there could be no possible common meeting ground for the two races. He could not conceive having a friendship or going tamely

57

to transact business with one of them. He looked furtively about to see how the others were taking the conversation, and found them following what was being said with calm acceptance of its ordinary nature.

It was evident Master Jenks was impressed with the fact that Joshua had met the Indian sachem in person. "Beyond doubt then," he remarked hopefully, "you managed to gather some notion of his present feelings toward us."

Joshua seemed to ponder on his reply. " 'Tis not easy to know the true feelings of an Indian, thee knows that," he said, speaking slowly and thoughtfully. "But of this much I'm sure. Metacom knows we distrust him—and that is a grave danger. From what I've seen here in my years in the colonies and from what I've read, I've learned one thing about the Indian. He reflects the attitude of the white man toward him. Where he has been given just treatment, friendship, and trust, he has returned them in full measure. Where not—" He broke off with a significant shrug, then in a moment continued, "Should trouble come here, 'twill be of our own making."

While Joshua was speaking, the other man's face had hardened into lines of settled opposition. "I could differ with you as to that, my friend; but I won't." He gave a short laugh of pointed meaning. "I've argued with others of your kind as to the proper way to treat Indians since I've been in this free-for-all Plantation." He gathered up his reins to show he was about to depart and, as Joshua opened his lips to reply, silenced him with a gesture. "Spare your breath, Master Mapes. Did we talk from now till doomsday we could ne'er see eye to eye."

He raised his hand in farewell and backed his horse away from the doorstep. But, as he turned to ride away, he added over his shoulder, "Still, were I in your place, Friend Mapes, I'd take a fool's advice and keep my family within doors the next few days." With that he rode off down the trail.

Joshua stood looking sorrowfully after the retreating figure. "There's a prime example of our time," he said at length with a sigh. "A righteous man, kindly in the main, but filled with hates and distrust of his fellows."

"Aye," added Naomi, speaking for the first time since the visitor's arrival, "and sowing seed from which all of us here may have a bitter harvest to reap."

Jonathan's concern was of a more immediate nature and, now that the reason for restraint was removed, it burst out violently. "And spoilin' the bayberry bee, what's more—the pesky scare-cat! Like as not most of the folk will credit his tale and not dare to leave their dooryards. There'll be no one at the bee and 'twill be no fun at all, picking alone."

His father patted his shoulder consolingly. "There, there, son, thee should not take such a doleful view. Some may come, and do they not," he ended with a twinkle, "perchance thee may find some nice little Indian boys out on the hills to pick with thee."

Naomi took the chandler's jest with utter seriousness. "Thee might for a fact, son," she told the boy, "and that would be fine for thee. An Indian lad could teach thee many useful things of which thy little white friends have no knowledge."

Patrick's face was blank with consternation. "You mean you are going to the bee in spite of all Master Jenks said?"

The family exchanged understanding glances.

59

"To be sure we are," replied Mistress Mapes in a matter-of-fact tone. "The bayberries have to be picked." Then, noting the boy's distressed expression, she added more gently, "Thee must not let thyself be frighted by such groundless talk, lad."

Patrick flushed uncomfortably and Hannah came quickly to his defense. " 'Tis no wonder he was frighted, Mother. Anyone who did not know the Indians as we do would have been." She turned to Patrick and continued reassuringly, "We have no fear of them because we have had them about us always and they have ne'er done us hurt."

Naomi gave a meaningful little laugh. "Counterwise, they have given us a sight of help. I'd no notion of how to manage in such a wilderness when we came here and I scarce know how I'd have made shift to feed my family but for what the Indian women taught me of native foods and cookery."

"And 'twas from them we learned basketry, too," added Hannah, "and how to make all manner of useful boxes from birch bark. There was an old squaw who taught me when I was just a wee thing and I grew to love her dearly."

"And don't forget splint brooms," put in Jonathan eagerly. "I think they're the best thing." He turned to Patrick to add, "I make 'em to trade for fishing hooks."

"Thee can see how we must feel," Hannah went on. "To us the Indians have been like good neighbor folks."

"That they have," the chandler agreed heartily. "In the near twenty years since my good wife and I came here into the Providence country we have known naught but kindness from them."

60

"But it has not been so elsewhere," faltered Patrick. "I read about the Pequot war in Connecticut."

Joshua's face became serious. "Aye, I know, son. That was bad. And 'twas especially so because 'twas a needless tragedy. The trouble that started it was of a white man's brewing and what followed might have been averted." He put his hands on Patrick's shoulders and looked earnestly into his face. " 'Twas men like Master Jenks that brought that war upon us. Thee knows the sort too well— men who feel their own kind must e'er be in the right and have no will to grant other folk the right to their own place and their own way of life." His gaze wandered off above the boy's head and he stood silent a moment, staring into space as though seeing things that were bitter to contemplate. But presently his eyes came back to Patrick's face again and he continued with a sigh, "Thee has seen thyself what miseries such a way of doing has caused in the Old World. Here in the New we are striving for a new way—a way of trust and tolerance. And surely we must start in that with the folk we found already here when we came. Else how should we expect they would tolerate us?" He gave a dubious little laugh. "So be we learn to live in peace and harmony with them, we might come in time to live peaceably with each other." He paused, smiling down at the lad and giving his shoulders a series of gentle little pats. "So pay no heed to the Master Jenks thee will meet all too oft and try instead to think of the Indians as folk just like ourselves—as neighbors we must trust."

Patrick did not reply at once. The chandler's words had thrown his mind into a distressing turmoil. But at length he made an uncertain effort to return his smile and answered in a troubled, doubtful voice, "I will, sir—I mean, at least, I'll try."

Naomi reached over and drew the boy gently from beneath her husband's hands. "Let the lad be for now," she urged. "He must have time to get used to our ways of thinking." Then, changing to a briskly practical tone, she continued, "We've no time to be standing here talking, in any case. Jonathan must get his meal ground and the pies we are to take to the bee on the morrow must be baked. There are other things for our mitchin-basket to be prepared as well, and so be Patrick is to have clothes to wear, I must finish my sewing."

Joshua touched her cheek in a fleeting caress. "Thee is right, wife—as thee near always is. Naught was yet mended by talk and we have our work to do." Then he turned to Jonathan and tapped him smartly on the shoulder. "Off with thee, lad, to thy grinding an thee wants pies on the morrow."

Jonathan ran off whistling to the barnyard and the rest of the family turned back into the house.

Patrick did not follow at once but stood gazing off over the western hills beyond which the Indians were encamped, his mind locked in a conflict between his long-nursed hatred of Old World intolerance and his own intolerant aversion to the natives of the New World into which he had come.

At length, in spite of all the Mapes family had said, the feeling that these American savages were creatures too vile to deserve the toleration of civilized men came uppermost. "Neighbors!" he said aloud in a tone of scathing contempt. Then at the sound of his own voice he stopped, aghast. It sounded for all the world as he remembered his father's voice when he spoke of people who differed from him in race and creed. It was the tone he always used when he spoke of that other Patrick, the Irish lad the new Patrick had so dearly loved.

5

ON THE BAYBERRY HILLS

PATRICK did not sleep well that night. He twisted and turned in his improvised bed on the settle, sitting bolt upright every now and again to listen intently. Indians might be prowling about out there in the darkness—and to save his life he could not make himself think of them as friends or neighbors. He fell into such troubled dreams, at length, that when he was wakened by a touch on his shoulder he started up with a cry, thinking he was being seized by a painted warrior.

"Mercy, boy, what ails thee?" said the voice of Mistress Mapes.

She was standing beside him, the light of the fire playing warmly over her plump figure and revealing the look of concern upon her face.

The boy gave an apologetic little laugh. "I must have been dreaming, I guess," he answered.

He cast a quick glance about the room. It was still dark; but the fire was blazing merrily and Hannah was laying the trestle board by candlelight.

"I'm sorry I gave thee such a start. I spoke to thee before I touched thee, but thee did not waken and, so be thee is going with us to pick bayberries today, thee must be getting up."

64

"Is it really time?" he asked, smothering a yawn. "It looks to be the middle of the night."

Hannah paused in the act of pouring milk into the noggins on the table. " 'Tis near dawn, sleepyhead," she told him, laughing, "and the trip to the hills about the bay where the bayberries grow is such a long one we should be on our way ere daybreak."

"Aye," added Naomi, "thee must make haste now. The clothes I fixed for thee are in the bed-chamber. Go in and put them on quickly, for Joshua and Jonathan will be in from the barn in a few moments; then we must have our meal at once."

Patrick scrambled up with his blankets about him and ran into the adjoining room. A candle was burning on a stool beside the bed and the garments were laid out upon it. Patrick picked them up and stood looking at them with a strange mixture of emotions. They were of coarse homespun cloth of a dark butternut brown and crude in cut and tailoring.

"My father's groom has better," he thought with a wry smile. Then he had a swift remembrance of the look on Naomi's face as she sat sewing on them. "Beyond doubt she robbed poor Master Mapes of one of his best suits to make them," he thought, and instantly the wry smile was gone.

He put them on with almost reverent hands and looked about for a mirror in which he could see himself. But there was none. He could only judge by the feel and what he could see looking down at them that they really fitted.

When he returned to the other room, Joshua and Jonathan had arrived and the entire family exclaimed together at his appearance.

65

Naomi was beaming with pride. "As I live, they fit him to a T. And their manly cut makes him look more a young man than the slip of a lad he seemed in his own things."

Joshua turned him about with a chuckle. "I didn't know with what a sightly young helper I'd provided myself."

Hannah said nothing but her eyes glowed with a shy delight.

Jonathan's look was one of disappointed disapproval. "He's sightly, sure enough," he admitted grudgingly, "but I liked him best in his boy's clothes."

Patrick longed to speak his thanks, but the words stuck in his throat. He could only look eloquently from the chandler to his wife and, as he slipped into his place at the table, he let his hand cover Naomi's a moment in a fleeting clasp of grateful affection.

She gave it a quick, warm pressure and for just an instant her eyes were misted. The next she said in her briskest manner, "Come now, be quick and finish thy meal."

It took but a few moments to dispatch the simple fare. Then, while the rest of the family took a hand in clearing up, Mistress Mapes put the last of the things for their midday meal into the hamper which had been packed the night before.

Joshua weighted it and then said to Jonathan, "Best bring Christopher up to the doorstep. Our women folk have provided such a feast 'twould be heavy to carry e'en as far as the barn."

Christopher was a venerable pack horse kept to transport the chandler's stock to market—a docile creature, fat with the loving pampering the family gave him and more like a dog than a horse in the affection he returned. Pat-

66

rick loved all animals and had fallen instant victim to Christopher's charms.

"Let me get him," he begged and, when permission was given, seized the lanthorn standing by the door and dashed off to the barn.

He found the horse already loaded with the baskets needed for picking the bayberries and bearing home the crop. Two deep hampers hung nearly to the ground on each side of the packsaddle, and a cluster of small baskets with their handles tied together was fastened at its back. He led the animal to the house and found the family waiting for him on the doorstep. The food hamper was secured on top of the saddle, and when that was done Christopher appeared to be a small mountain of baskets with a horse's head and hind quarters protruding from it and legs beneath.

The sky beyond the hills was gray with dawn by that time and the trail was faintly visible. So the lanthorn was put out and stowed away in one of the deep hampers in order that they might have it with them in case dark overtook them on the way back. And then they were ready to start.

The trail was so narrow they had to walk single file. Joshua took the lead, Naomi came next, then Hannah with Patrick close behind so he could talk to her as they went, and Jonathan brought up the rear leading Christopher. They were headed westward over the crest of the hill and, noting the fact, Patrick asked with interest if their way lay past Providence.

"The trail goes past there," Hannah told him, "but we leave it at the Great Falls and take a little foot trail that leads southward on this side of the river."

Patrick pricked up his ears at mention of the falls. "Is that the one where Master Jenks said the Indians were camped?" he asked.

"Aye, it is," answered Hannah. "And should the camp chance to be on this side of the river we'll go right past it. I hope it will be, for that would be such a fine chance for thee to see some Indians."

Patrick was not entirely sure he wanted it to be where they would pass it. The idea of seeing an Indian camp was exciting; but the thought of getting so close to the Indians themselves gave him a queer, creepy sensation up his spine.

It turned out they did pass the site of the camp. But there were no Indians there.

Joshua made a rapid survey of the deserted remains of the camp and announced that evidently the Indians had broken camp at dawn and moved on only a short time before. "The ashes of the camp fires are still warm," he remarked; then added in an amused tone, " 'Tis as I imagined. Master Jenks' 'goodly band' of Indians turns out to be but three families at the most. Or possibly one family unit made up of an old couple and two married children with families of their own."

"But how can you know the number like that, sir?" asked Patrick curiously.

"By the fact that they had three wigwams," replied the Quaker. He pointed to three odd-looking skeleton structures of conical shape made from pliable saplings set in the ground in a circle and then bent over so their tops came together and could be tied firmly in place. "Those pole structures form the framework of their temporary lodges. They are completed by being covered with mats woven of grasses or rush which the women carry with them. 'Abackquosinash' they call them in their own tongue."

He stood looking about with an expression of brooding thought. "Thousands of Indians have camped here, on this very spot most like, or very near here. For this place has been the great fishing grounds of many tribes for longer than anyone knows. Before the whites settled all about they used to have great yearly festivals here at the time when the salmon comes up the river to spawn. No doubt this group stopped here for a last bit of fishing ere going on to their homes in the hills."

Patrick tried to picture them at their fishing and living peacefully in their wigwams—but he couldn't. All he had read had been of Indians on the warpath and he could only think of them so. He breathed a sigh of relief when they left the camp behind.

Just beyond it they left the trail, as Hannah had said they would, and took a faintly marked little path leading southward.

"We call it Bayberry Trail," Hannah told the boy, "because 'tis scarce used at all except by the folk when they go to pick the berries."

For a time it ran along beside the river. Then the river's course seemed to bear away from it and it plunged into dense woods and, for what seemed hours to Patrick, wound in and out among trees so tall and so close together that when the sun was high in the sky they only knew it by the fact that here and there motes of sunshine, like golden coins, seemed falling down through the thick foliage. But gradually the trees grew smaller and thinned out enough so that the sun came through in bands of sunlight slanting down through them like paths of misty gold. After a while those dwindled to a sparse, stunted growth and presently the little party emerged onto low, treeless hills rolling down to an expanse of blue water.

Similar hills rose on the opposite shore and beyond those forest rolled away to the west. There was a salt tang in the air which told that the sea was not far distant.

"Oh," cried Patrick, "is it Narragansett Bay?"

Joshua turned round to smile back at him. "Hardly that. 'Tis just the first small inlet. More properly it belongs to the Great Salt River which connects the Bay with Providence. The Bay itself is still some miles south of here."

"You can smell the sea though," insisted the boy, drawing in delighted drafts of the bracing air. "But there's another smell beside," he added, sniffing questioningly. "Something sweet and fresh—a bit like lavender, only better."

The observation brought a pleased expression to Hannah's face. "I hoped thee would notice it," she said. "That is the fragrance of bayberry. Look," she added, making a gesture which took in all the low hill in front of them, "as far as thee can see is covered with the bushes. It always grows thus—on hills close to salt water. It seems to thrive in sandy soil and salty air."

The hillslope just in front of them was thick with the glossy-leaved bushes. Patrick and Hannah ran to the first of them and Patrick saw that it was loaded with masses of small gray-green berries. He gathered a handful and held them to his nose.

"Um—um, what a nice smell!" he exclaimed. Then he fell to examining the berries. The thing that gave them the grayish tinge was a delicate, frost-like coating of silvery white, lightly covering the green of the berry. "They look as though each one had been dusted with some fine white powder," he commented.

"That is the wax from which we make the candles," Hannah told him. "Scrape off a bit with thy fingernail."

He did as she bade him and noted that where the white powder came off, the berry was glossy green beneath and that the powder gave his finger a waxy feeling.

"But it must take bushels of them to yield wax sufficient for a candle," he said, amazed. "And how in the world can you scrape off the wax from each berry?"

There was a twinkle in Hannah's eyes as though she were trying not to laugh. But she had no chance to reply, for at that moment the rest of the party came up and diverted her attention.

Jonathan was looking disgustedly about, scanning the hills in every direction. "Wasn't this the place where the others that were going on the picking were to join us?" he asked with pointed sarcasm.

His mother admitted reluctantly that it was.

His eyes went round the circle of the landscape once more. "Not a livin' body here," he commented; then added with conviction, "I knew 'twould be so."

But Naomi would not give up hope so easily. "Some may have gone on to the place where we spread our tuck-a-muck each year and be waiting there for us," she suggested. "Perchance we should go there and look for them before we start picking."

Jonathan gave a scornful grunt. "There won't be anybody there. I'm mortal sure o' that. But we could go and look anyway." Then an idea seemed to occur to him which made his face brighten. "And as long as we'll be at our eating place, why couldn't we eat? I'm near starving now."

"And me as well," laughed Joshua. "I've a notion we could all enjoy our meal as well now as later—and be the better for our picking."

The suggestion was a more than welcome one to Patrick. He had not eaten much at the hurried early morning meal and was feeling famished. But he was also so weary that the prospect of more walking was uninviting. " 'Twould suit me mightily to eat," he remarked doubtfully, "but I'm near the end of my rope for walking farther till I rest a bit."

"The place is just over the brow of the hill," Hannah told him encouragingly. " 'Tis the best of camping spots because there's a fine spring with a nice clump of trees about it."

The picture gave the tired boy new heart. He agreed he thought he could make it, and the party started on again.

It was not necessary for them to walk single file on the open hilltop, so now Joshua and Naomi went ahead together and the three young people followed side by side.

When they were nearly at the crest of the hill Joshua stopped suddenly, sniffing the breeze with his head raised like a hound.

"What is it, husband?" asked Naomi.

"Wood smoke," replied Joshua. "Don't the rest of you smell it?"

They all sniffed and agreed they did.

Naomi beamed with satisfaction. "Now, see. Some of our good neighbors did come, after all. Come, quickly. They will be weary waiting for us."

They hurried on and as they breasted the hilltop saw

there were indeed people beside a camp fire near the clump of trees. But they were not the neighbors Naomi had expected.

"Indians!" exclaimed Jonathan in delighted excitement. "Oh, good!"

"A family of them," added Hannah, her voice warm with pleasure.

And so it was. There was a father and mother, a girl somewhat younger than Hannah, a boy about Jonathan's age, and a baby hung from a low branch of one of the trees in a papoose carrier. The older children had evidently run to their parents when they detected the approach of strangers and the four now stood in a close group facing the intruders, just as the Mapes family was apt to stand when confronting outsiders.

A wigwam like those at the deserted camp—except that its conical frame was neatly covered with mats—stood among the trees behind them. Baskets, earthen pots, and other articles designed for primitive housekeeping, clustered about its open doorway, spoke eloquently of the domestic life it sheltered. A camp fire burned near by where a meal was evidently in preparation. An ingenious grill, made of green saplings resting on a frame supported at the corners by four forked sticks of green wood, covered the coals at one end, and upon it a great fish with the head and tail still on it was stretched out roasting. At the other a great kettle, from which rose a most savory odor, was suspended over the blaze in a sapling tripod.

Joshua and his party had halted instinctively and the two families stood silently appraising each other. All but Patrick were only waiting to see what sort of a greeting each group would give the other. Patrick was absorbed in making rapid mental notes on these examples of the race about which he had read such horrifying accounts and in hastily revising his ideas about Indians.

The descriptions encountered in his reading had pictured Indian braves as ferocious-looking creatures with hideous faces grotesquely painted and naked bodies decked with feathers and barbarous ornaments. This Indian was not painted and he did not look in the least ferocious. He was naked to the waist, to be sure, revealing muscles that filled the boy with envy and red-brown skin that glistened in the sunshine like burnished copper. But his limbs were clad in hip-high buckskin leggins held up by loops passed over a handsome beaded belt. Other than that his only ornament was a single tall, straight feather thrust into the long hair twisted at the back of his head into a sort of filleted knot. The forepart of his head was shaven with only one small tuft of short hair left standing erect upon the crown, and there was something majestic about the domed structure of his skull. His bearing had a kind of regal dignity and his face an austere nobility. All in all his appearance struck the boy as being really imposing.

The squaws mentioned in the books he had read had been described as fat and repulsively dirty. This Indian woman was girlishly slender. Her short deerhide skirt and sleeveless jerkin were clean and not untastefully ornamented with embroidery of beads and tiny shells. Her black hair was glossy and neatly ordered into two braids which hung one over either shoulder.

The children were just as they had been pictured—almost entirely naked. The girl wore nothing but a briefly scant skirt of stuff woven from grasses. The boy only a strip of cloth passed over a thong tied about his waist and left to hang down in front like a diminutive apron. But someway it seemed fitting their little brown bodies should be bare like that.

The woman had a look of shy docility and the children a timid sweetness. The father's attitude as he stood beside his little brood bespoke pride in his family, affection, and protectiveness. The effect of the family group against the background of its home and fireside was that of a peculiarly gentle domesticity.

Patrick found himself touched by it almost to tenderness. Once again the word "neighbors" formed in his mind. But this time, had he spoken it aloud, it would have been in a very different tone.

"Aye," he thought with a reluctant, incredulous acceptance, "these could really seem such."

6

PAUCOTTAUWAT, THE GREAT DEER

THE two groups stood thus in silence for what seemed to Patrick a very long moment. Then Joshua turned to the rest of his party and said in a low tone, "Wait here a bit while I go ahead and speak to them." With that he walked forward a short distance, raised his arm in salutation, and called out some words which sounded to Patrick like, "Wha' cheer, Netop!"

He looked questioningly at Hannah. "What was that your father said?" he asked.

" 'What cheer, friend,' " she replied. " 'Tis the accepted greeting of friendship between the Indians of this district and white people because 'twas so the Indians greeted Roger Williams when he first appeared in their territory." She had leaned close to the boy and spoken in a rapid undertone, for the two families were close enough so that ordinary conversation would have been audible.

The familiar greeting brought a look of relief to the Indian's face. He raised his arm in a similar greeting and called back a brief phrase which was evidently a friendly answer.

"He says, 'Greetings, friends.' " Hannah interpreted.

Joshua answered something in the same language, advancing as he did so until he stood close before the Indian.

76

"He is speaking Algonquin to them," the girl explained. "He has learned something of the tongue from Roger Williams."

The Indian's face broke into a smile. He turned to his wife and said a few words in a pleased tone and then back to speak to Joshua. Patrick could not distinguish what he was saying—but it did not sound like Algonquin. In fact it had a strangely familiar ring.

He stared at Hannah in puzzled amazement. "Am I crazed?" he demanded.

Hannah shook her head, her eyes twinkling with amusement. "Thee is quite in thy right mind. He is speaking English. Many of the young men do. After all they have grown up with the English all about them."

It seemed incredible yet, obviously, the Indian and Joshua were enjoying a very cordial chat. Presently Joshua turned and beckoned the rest of his party to join him. They went forward and when they reached the other group the Indian gave them a formal but friendly smile of welcome.

"All folk of him welcome," he said. "To him because he speak Indian we give welcome of brother."

Joshua had evidently introduced himself and accounted for their presence in what might be regarded as the Indian's dooryard. Now he first presented Naomi and then all the others by name.

The Indian acknowledged the introductions with grave politeness and reciprocated with introductions of his own.

"My name Paucottauwat," he announced with almost oppressive dignity. He nodded toward the woman beside him. "Wife, Qunneke." Then he touched the shoulder of the little girl. "Squasese, Moosquin."

"Ah," exclaimed Joshua, "my brother is honored with a noble name." He turned to the others to explain. "He is named for the great buck deer, one of the most kingly of all the beasts." He paused, and it seemed to Patrick that it was to hide some amusement, then went on, "Fittingly his wife is called 'The Doe' and his little daughter, 'Faun.' "

Jonathan had been waiting eagerly to learn the name of the boy and, since it had not been announced, he could curb his impatience no longer. He pointed his stubby finger at the Indian lad, demanding bluntly, "What's his name?"

The Indian's oppressive dignity relaxed for the first time. There was a smile of benign amusement on his face as he looked down at the white boy and his voice had changed to that of a kindly, indulgent father. "Him no name yet," he replied. "Indian boy must win name. For now call him 'Wemat,' same you say brother."

Naomi nodded a brisk approval. "And a most fitting name it is for a little lad with an older sister." Her warm smile gathered the two children into her affections and then moved on to include Qunneke.

The dark eyes of the Indian mother smiled back a shy reply. She had not been able to understand the words of the other woman but her smile carried a message of universal motherhood—and that she understood perfectly. She laid a timid hand on her husband's arm and said something to him which was evidently a request or suggestion.

Paucottauwat bent his head in sober agreement; then turning to the others said in a more friendly tone than he had yet used to them, "Qunneke say we have much good fish and big pot seekguttahash ready cooked. She ask you eat with us."

Patrick recalled the bountiful repast packed in the hamper Christopher was carrying which Hannah and Naomi had prepared with so much anticipation, and looked from one to the other to see how they were receiving the invitation. For his own part, he found himself eager to share the meal of the Indian family; but he suspected from Naomi's expression that she was casting about for a courteous way of phrasing a refusal. She had no chance to make it, however, for Joshua stopped her with an almost imperceptible warning touch on the arm, then turned to Paucottauwat with a flowery expression of thanks and acceptance.

Evidently Naomi had no intention of relinquishing the enjoyment of the food they had brought themselves, but she took her cue from her husband and, giving her Indian host a deprecating smile, added, "We have some poor fare we brought with us to keep us from hunger until we could reach home again and—poor as it is—perchance thee and thy family will partake of some of that as well."

The Indian accepted with the same flowery phraseology Joshua had used. By that time Patrick had begun to feel that social intercourse with Indians had almost the exactions of associations with royalty.

The matter of having a meal together being arranged at length, the hamper was lifted down from Christopher's packsaddle and Jonathan and Wemat were sent off to tether the horse to graze. Then, while Qunneke took the pot from the fire and set it on the ground in the center of a cleared space that evidently served the Indians as a dining table, and transferred the fish from the grill to a mat of finely woven grass to place beside it, Naomi and Hannah unpacked the hamper and set out the food they had brought. The Indians exclaimed in admiring wonder at the pies, but all the other food seemed familiar to them.

When all the food was set out Moosquin ran to the wigwam and brought a pile of wooden bowls and a spoon of wood or horn for each person and placed them on the ground beside the pot. The boys had returned by that time and Qunneke signified that the meal was ready. They all sat down in a circle about the food, Qunneke handed a bowl and a spoon to each, and everyone helped himself from the central dishes.

Patrick followed suit and noted that the dish from the pot was a mixture of corn and beans stewed together with bits of meat.

Hannah had served herself also by that time, and when she saw what the dish was she gave an exclamation of pleased recognition. "Oh, 'tis succotash," she cried, "the thing I like best of all."

All the Indians broke into a laugh at the girl's English corruption of the name of their native dish and then Paucottauwat asked with evident pleasure, "You cook the seekguttahash, too?"

"To be sure," replied Naomi; "one of thy women taught me years ago."

"Aye," added Joshua, "that, like all the other numerous foods prepared from maize, is one of the Indian's many gifts to the white race." He smiled warmly at the Indian. "My race owes thine a great debt. Were it not for the fact that thy people taught the first Pilgrim settlers how to plant, grow, and use thy native grain, they would have perished of starvation."

Patrick expected the Indian to show flattered gratification at the tribute. Instead he cast a sharp sidelong glance at Joshua and then looked away, a dark shadow gathering on his brows. Presently his dark eyes came back to Joshua's face and there was a kind of challenge in them. "Might have been better so," he said bluntly in a voice that had grown hard as flint.

Quick understanding and sympathy flashed into Joshua's face. " 'Tis no wonder thee feels so, my brother," he said gently, "but e'en had those settlers perished 'twould have made no difference to thy people in the end. In fact it might have gone much worse with them. Other white men would have come and few would have dealt as fairly with thy race as the Pilgrims."

Paucottauwat made no reply but sat gazing off across the bay in brooding silence. The stern bitterness of his expression sent a chill through Patrick. The boy glanced anxiously at Joshua, hoping he would say something to placate the Indian. But the sight of the other man's unhappiness seemed to have smitten the chandler dumb himself. He was gazing at the Indian with an expression of poignant, hopeless sorrow as though he knew exactly what he was feeling and realized nothing could be done to make it otherwise.

A pall seemed to fall over the entire party and everyone stopped eating until Qunneke gently reminded her husband that his food was growing cold. The meal was resumed in an awkward hush and went on in a constrained silence for some time. But the mellowing influence of good food gradually overcame Paucottauwat's gloom and by the time they were ready to attack the pies he was chatting genially.

Naomi had been so occupied with her sewing the afternoon before that Hannah had baked the pies alone. It was her first effort in unsupervised pastry-cooking and she had been awaiting the moment when a verdict would be passed upon them with some trepidation. Paucottauwat, at least, seemed to find them excellent. When he had consumed three pieces with evident relish, he turned to Naomi with a smile of beaming commendation. "You make something much good to eat," he told her in a flattering tone.

Naomi shook her head and pointed to Hannah. " 'Twas not I that made them. 'Twas the little daughter there."

The Indian turned his smile upon the girl. "Squasese can make a thing so good!" he exclaimed in pleased surprise.

Hannah was pink with modest pride. " 'Tis nice thee found them good," she faltered. "I am but learning as yet."

Paucottauwat still beamed upon her. "For making a thing so good squasese should have reward," he declared. He seemed to reflect a moment, then smiled as though an idea had come to him and, turning to Moosquin, said something to her in their own language.

Moosquin nodded happily and, jumping up with a shy smile at the other girl, ran to the wigwam and began rummaging about among the household equipment that stood beside it.

Her father rose from his place also, went over to the camp fire, and squatting on his heels beside it began raking a small bed of coals together under one corner of the grill as though in preparation for some special task of cookery.

Presently Moosquin returned carrying a small, close-woven basket in one hand and an odd-looking implement in the other. It was about the shape and size of a warming pan. But the pan part, instead of being of metal, was a very openwork basket woven of green willow withes and fastened to a handle made of a green sapling.

Paucottauwat beckoned to Hannah. "Come see, squasese," he said, much in the tone of a child with some delightful secret to impart.

Hannah got up and went to him. He said a few words to Moosquin and she handed him the odd implement, then held out the covered basket to Hannah.

"Yo commeish, Hannah," she said timidly but still plainly delighted at what she was doing.

Hannah did not understand the meaning of the words and cast an inquiring glance at Paucottauwat.

"She says, 'Give you this,' " he explained.

A flush of pleasure spread up to Hannah's smooth chestnut hair. "Oh, thank you both, so much," she faltered, taking the basket and starting to examine it. " 'Tis a lovely basket."

"Basket only for hold real reward," Paucottauwat told her. "Squasese look inside."

The others had risen curiously and crowded about to see what the basket contained. Hannah raised the lid carefully and revealed pearly white kernels of some sort of grain heaped to its top. They were smaller than the kernel of ordinary maize, more oblong and pointed and had a glossy, almost translucent finish.

Joshua took out a few grains to examine. "Plainly 'tis maize of some kind," he said, "but of a sort I have ne'er seen ere this."

Paucottauwat had placed the open-work basket on the grill over his carefully prepared bed of coals and he now pointed to it with an air of delighted mystery. "Same in here," he announced. "Watch."

Hannah noticed for the first time then that the bottom of the basket was covered with the same pearly white kernels. Paucottauwat crouched beside the fire shaking it back and forth over the heat with an intent and serious expression.

Nothing happened for a time; but finally one of the kernels moved slightly as though it were alive. The next moment there was a sharp little report and it leaped upward, bursting open as it did so, revealing a fleecy, snow-white heart and turning the burst shell backward in little points like the petals of a flower. In an instant another kernel did likewise, then another, and soon the whole basketful was popping merrily and the basket looked as though it contained a miniature snowstorm.

"Look'it, look'it," cried Jonathan, hopping about in wild excitement. "They're all of 'em popping open!"

When the last kernel had exploded Paucottauwat took the basket from the fire and, after raising the lid, held it out to Hannah. "Good to eat," he told her. "Taste him."

The girl took the basket but before tasting its contents herself started passing the strange new food about to the others.

Joshua took a few of the snowy kernels which in their new state were easily four times as large as their originals, but instead of eating them began examining them with keen interest. "Now, as I live," he commented, holding one up between finger and thumb, "it has almost the semblance of a tiny flower."

The Indian's face broke into a delighted smile. "That its name," he said. "Indian see look like flower long time since and call 'maize that flower.' "

"Oh," exclaimed Hannah, "what a pretty name! I shall

ne'er call my popping maize by any other."

When the basket reached Patrick, he could not contain his curiosity for politeness' sake, and bit at once into one of the kernels. It was delightfully crunchy and had a delicious, sweet, nut-like flavor. "Um-m-m," he exclaimed. "Good!"

He had taken almost no part in the talk up to that moment, contenting himself with being a silent but interested observer, and his Indian hosts had seemed to pay little attention to him. Now Paucottauwat cast him an approving smile, then, nodding toward him, remarked to Joshua, "Son, he knows good to eat."

The chandler laid his arm about the boy's shoulder. "The lad is not my son," he replied, then added as though making an announcement of especial interest, "He is my ward. 'Nulloquaso,' as thy people say."

His tone made Patrick look up into his face in quick question. It sounded as though having a ward were something the Indian would regard as a great piece of good fortune.

And evidently it was so. For an expression of new respect came into Paucottauwat's face. He seemed to be looking Patrick over appraisingly for a moment, then he nodded as though in approval of what he had seen and turned to Joshua to ask, "You adopt him?"

Joshua gave the boy's shoulders a warm little squeeze. "Aye," he answered heartily, "I adopt him into Mapes tribe."

Patrick remembered then that in the book about the Pequot War he had read there had been several references to a custom among the Indians of adopting the most promising of the children taken as prisoners and rearing

them with every care and honor so that when they reached
adult life they would feel themselves identified with the
tribe into which they had been adopted and add to its
numbers and strength. He recalled that it was felt a great
honor to be the foster parent of a lad who was a potential
tribal warrior, and that if the boy became a great brave,
the foster parent was always held in especial respect.

In spite of himself Patrick found himself accepting the
Indian valuation of his place in the Mapes household. He
no longer felt himself a poor waif taken in out of the good-
ness of their hearts. There was no reason, he thought, why
he should not prove just as much value to Joshua and his
family as adopted Indian lads did to their foster parents.
His thin shoulders straightened. His head went up with
new pride. Deep in his heart he registered a silent vow that
it should be so.

A blanket was spread beneath one of the trees apart
from the domestic activities where it was evident Paucottauwat was accustomed to take his masculine ease after
meals while the women folk cleared the food away. He
nodded toward it now, smiling a dignified invitation first
to Joshua and then to Patrick. "We talk now," he announced.

Patrick realized that he was included in the invitation
because, as the honored pupil of a guest, it was his right to
sit by and listen to the talk of men. He took his place on
the blanket with a feeling of dignified self-esteem.

The Indian produced a tobacco pipe with a small, square
bowl of carved stone and a long reed stem and filled it
with tobacco from a deerhide pouch at his belt. Moosquin
came running with a brand from the fire with which to
light it as though it were a duty to which she was accus-

tomed, handed it to her father, and then ran back to join the women. Paucottauwat took a few puffs at the pipe and then handed it gravely to Joshua.

Patrick had seen no tobacco in the chandler's house and had assumed that, like most Quakers, Joshua did not use it. If that were true he permitted no such fact to be evident to the Indians. He accepted the pipe with equal gravity, took a puff or two, and returned it to his host. They smoked thus in solemn silence for a little, passing the pipe back and forth, then Joshua inquired politely if Paucottauwat expected to remain long in his present camp.

The Indian shook his head. "Another sun we move on to Great Falls. Stay there two suns then go to home village." And he mentioned a location by its Indian name.

"Ah," said Joshua, "in the heart of the Massasoit country. I take it then thee must be of the Wampanoag tribe, the same as thy great sachem."

Paucottauwat gave assent with a serious nod. Then he added with quiet pride, "Cousin to Sachem Metacomet."

The mention of the relationship made Patrick steal a swift glance at the chandler. The conversation he had heard the day before had made him feel that, above all things, it was imperative the white settlers should know the state of the sachem's feelings toward them. This happy encounter with one of his close relatives seemed to provide an unbelievably fortunate chance to find out at first hand. He expected Joshua to take immediate advantage of it and to begin plying the Indian with questions as to his cousin's attitude toward white men. But Joshua did nothing of the kind. He made the flattering comment that Paucottauwat's bearing had already led him to suspect his connection with the royal house—and then dismissed the matter of the relationship altogether. He told of his own meetings with Metacomet and spoke feelingly of the chief's great father Massasoit and what his friendship had meant to the white colonists.

Patrick experienced a feeling of baffled impatience. Was it possible, he thought, that the Quaker was going to let such a rare opportunity slip by without seizing it?

Paucottauwat had been politely attentive, but he had confined his responses to nods and a word or two now and again, and showed no signs of wishing to assume a more active part in the talk. So Joshua went on to speak of the peace treaty Massasoit had made with the Pilgrims and how faithfully it had been kept by both red men and white.

Patrick saw then where the talk was leading and realized he was witnessing an example of the diplomacy necessary in dealing with an Indian. But he noted that Paucottauwat seemed also to suspect where the chandler was trying to lead the conversation, for his expression of polite attention had hardened gradually into a look of stony reserve.

"But now," Joshua ended with a deprecating shrug, "there are some hereabouts so foolish as to say thy noble cousin is angry at his white brothers."

The Indian made no direct reply to that statement but answered guardedly, "Things have been done that have wounded my cousin's heart. His faith has been doubted and the muskets of his warriors taken away."

The Quaker gave an understanding, sympathetic nod. "I know," he replied, "that was not good. But the law-makers at Plymouth are frighted. Some say thy cousin's wrath against the unscrupulous whites that have stooped so low as to play upon his generosity and lead him on to barter away so much of his land for worthless trifles is so great he is but waiting for a chance to break the peace pledge and take the warpath against us."

A blistering contempt kindled in the Indian's eyes. "My cousin not care for land," he declared. "There is much land—" He waved his arm about in a sweeping circle to take in the landscape of rolling hills and bay and more hills again on the opposite shore. "—enough for all. He cares that when white man have it he not willing Indian live his own way. He not like his people have white man's ways. He not want them taught white man's God better than Indian's Great Spirit."

Patrick caught his breath with shock and surprise. Those last words of the Indian's had struck home to an old tender spot. It had never occurred to him that he might find the same kind of mistaken religious zeal he had seen breeding hatred and strife in Europe at work doing the same thing here in the American wilderness. He understood now why Paucottauwat's face had worn that look of bitter unhappiness as he had gazed off across the bay.

He was so engrossed in his own thoughts for a time that he lost track of the talk of the others. But presently he became aware of Joshua's voice speaking and realized its tone had changed completely. He glanced quickly at the Quaker and saw that the look on his face had also changed. The mask of diplomacy had fallen from it leaving it shining with a clear light of truth. He was speaking with deep feeling of man's right to worship as he saw fit. He was denouncing his own race for violating the Indian's right to the same privilege.

The boy glanced furtively at Paucottauwat to see how he was taking this unexpected turn in the conversation.

The mask of diplomacy had fallen from his face as well. He was staring at the Quaker with utter, unconcealed amazement.

"You not like your preachers make praying Indians of my people?" he demanded incredulously.

Joshua smote the earth beside him in a gesture of violent denial. "Why should I?" he protested. "I am what men call a Quaker. At bottom the faith of my people is the same as thine. We both look to a Divine Spirit for help and guidance. Thy people look to hear Him speak to them from the hills and the sky. Mine listen to hear Him speak within their own hearts."

There was such vehement sincerity in his voice and manner that gradually Paucottauwat's expression of doubtful amazement changed to a look of acceptance and delighted wonder. By the time the Quaker ceased speaking the last of the Indian's defenses were down. His face was as soft and open as a child's. "From now on shall give my brother new name," he said softly. "Shall call him 'Taupowaw,' the Wise-speaker."

Joshua accepted the tribute with a smile of tremulous gratitude and Patrick saw that, for the moment, it was beyond his power to answer in words. They all sat silent for a space. At first the Quaker's mind seemed to have strayed far from the problems of the colonists; but, at length, a thoughtful look came into his eyes which told the boy he was going back over what had been said, drawing conclusions and deciding on a course of action.

"Thee has done thy brother the honor to call him wise," he said presently, "so perchance thee will hark to his words and heed his council." He paused an instant to give the Indian an opportunity to reply, but Paucottauwat seemed to have no intention of doing so, so he went on again. "From things thee has said I see plainly that those who say thy cousin has a grievance against his white brothers are not as foolish as I thought. He has the most potent of all grievances—and I much fear dire things may come of it."

The old reserve dropped like a veil over the openness of the Indian's face. The Quaker's expression showed he had noted the fact; but, notwithstanding, he continued with undaunted earnestness. "Thee must believe me when I say the welfare of thy people is as close to my heart as that of my own race, and I tell thee truly that should anything move thy cousin to take the warpath against the whites no good will come of it. His warriors are no longer a match for the English. Remember what happened to the Pequots. The blood of both races would be spilled to no purpose. I charge thee solemnly to counsel thy cousin against the folly of attempting to regain his power by war with the whites."

Paucottauwat stirred uneasily and glanced from side to side as though seeking an escape from the Quaker's clear gaze. "My cousin not heed counsel of humble relative," he said with stubborn defensiveness.

Joshua made a gesture of impatience. "Then white men who have the good of both races at heart must counsel him. Promise me that should thee see his mind turning toward war thee will come at once and tell me." He went on hastily to describe the whereabouts of his house so the Indian could find it. "E'en do thee have to come by night thee can find the place," he ended, "for there is always a candle alight in the window."

But Paucottauwat did not promise. For a time he did

not even reply, but sat looking at Joshua, his face dark with the misery of conflict between his new attachment to the Quaker and some feeling of old loyalty to his own race. At length, as though making a promise to himself, if not to Joshua, he replied in a strangely gentle tone, "Paucottauwat not forget Taupowaw and his folk."

The Quaker leaned back with a smothered sigh of defeat. He had accepted the impossibility of getting the Indian to commit himself farther. In a moment he turned to Patrick with a wry smile. "Well, lad," he said, "so be we are to get our bayberries picked today we had best be about it." He gave another sigh, looked back at Paucottauwat, and added with quiet finality, "We must be going now, my friend."

The Indian rose at once with evident relief. Joshua and Patrick followed suit and the three stood in awkward silence. Then Joshua held out his hand in the English manner at parting. "Farewell, Paucottauwat," he said simply.

Paucottauwat returned the handclasp in the white man's way. As the two men stood thus in the old posture of friendship and fraternity, all difference in race seemed obliterated. But when the handclasp ended he stepped back with the old oppressive Indian dignity and raised his hand in the Indian gesture of farewell.

"Hawunsheck, netompauog (Farewell, friends)," he said, reverting to his own language. Once more he was all Indian. He was Paucottauwat, the Great Deer, cousin of Metacomet, chief of the Wampanoags and Grand Sachem of all the Pokanokets.

7

WAX FROM THE BAYBERRY

QUNNEKE, Moosquin, and Wemat had insisted on joining in the picking, so in spite of the time consumed by the talk with Paucottauwat the hampers Christopher bore home at the close of the day were filled to the brim with bayberries.

"Our crop surely profited from meeting the Indians," Joshua remarked laughingly to the boys as they were unloading the packsaddle in the barn by lanthorn light. "All the red folk are deft with their hands and our three friends did so well for us that we've a store of berries sufficient to yield a goodly lot of wax."

The comment reminded Patrick of the puzzling problem of how the task of removing the wax from the berries was to be accomplished, and when he had stowed the hampers away in the tool room he put the question to the chandler.

But Joshua would not tell him. "Thee will see on the morrow," he answered instead, adding in a jesting tone, "and all too soon to please thee most like. For we will have thee up at crack o' day to start with the work."

He was as good as his word. The next morning the family sat down to their breakfast of corn meal porridge in the gray light of the early dawn. Once more it was a hurried meal. The rest of the family finished as quickly as possible; but Jonathan seemed dazed with sleepiness and when the others were done was still dallying over his trencher.

His father tapped him on the arm with some impatience. "Come, come, son. Make haste and eat up thy samp so thee can run out to the woods and cut us a lug pole."

Jonathan grinned up at him over his suspended spoon. "'Tis cut already," he announced with evident complacency. "I got a fine one on our way home last night. I left it out by the fire place."

"Well, I declare!" exclaimed the chandler. "Thee showed a foresight worthy of thy mother. I should have thought of doing that myself. Now we can get our fire going at once."

He rose from the table and Jonathan bolted his last spoonful of porridge and scrambled up to join him.

Patrick had no idea what it was they were planning to do, but it was evidently something related to the work of removing the wax from the bayberries, so he jumped up also, asking eagerly, "Am I to come too, sir?"

"What else?" answered Joshua heartily. "Thee is now the chandler's apprentice. Thee can start thy day's work by helping Jonathan get out the pots we will need."

Mistress Mapes gave vent to a roguish little chuckle. "Look behind thee by the water barrel," she told her husband.

The chandler glanced quickly round at a row of six huge iron kettles standing beside the barrel and then back at his wife with his brows raised and his head cocked in question.

"I got them out first thing when I got up so they'd be

96

ready," she replied in answer to the look.

Joshua gave her chin a playful pinch. "So thee and Jonathan are both ahead of me now," he observed, laughing. He crossed to the water barrel and taking the gourd dipper began dipping water into the kettles.

Mistress Mapes had risen from the table herself by that time and was briskly gathering the empty noggins together. "I'll come out myself as soon as I've red up after the meal and bring the paddles and baskets. Hannah'll be there in a jiffy with the fire shovel."

Joshua paused in his dipping to look over his shoulder at Hannah. "Don't make it too short a jiffy, daughter," he advised. "We'll need time to get the pots hung and the fire laid and we don't want our coals dying out ere we're ready to use them." He picked up two of the kettles and nodded to the others. "Come, boys, take two apiece of these and we'll be on our way."

Patrick obeyed, still completely at sea as to what the preparations were for and where they were going. It turned out their destination was the barnyard. On previous visits there the boy had noticed a circle of fire-blackened stones between two stout poles with crotched tops which were set into the earth so the crotches were at exactly the same height. Evidently they were for the purpose of supporting another pole above a fire and he had wondered then to what use such an outdoor fire was put. Now Joshua led the way directly to it. They all put down their kettles and Jonathan ran to pick up a newly cut sapling lying on the ground near by.

"Look, Father," he said proudly, handing it to the chandler, "isn't it a fine one? The hickory's near as hard as iron."

97

Joshua weighed it in his hand with a pleased expression, then holding it out endwise before his face sighted along its length with one eye closed. "And near as straight as an iron one too," he commented. "In short, son," he ended, lowering the sapling and smiling down at the boy with an air of triumph, " 'tis a perfect lug pole."

Jonathan glowed with pride. "A pole the like of that won't break and spill our wax in the fire, will it, Father?"

"Nay, I'm sure it won't," the chandler answered abstractedly. He had taken his jackknife from his pocket and was holding the sapling up against the upright poles to measure where the crotches would come on it. Having made sure of the spots, he marked them carefully and cut grooves so the pole would set snugly down into the crotches. That done, he fitted the lug pole into place and tested its firmness by swinging on it as though it were a turning bar. When he had satisfied himself that all was as it should be, he turned to Jonathan again. "Run along now, son," he commanded, "and fetch brush and wood for the fire."

Jonathan dashed to the woodpile and Patrick, all anxiety to be helping, asked eagerly, "Shouldn't I go and bring wood too, sir?"

Joshua shook his head, smiling reassuringly at the anxious boy. "Thee can help me hang the pots," he told him. "Run into the tool room and bring the trammels. Thee will find them hanging on the wall with the garden tools."

Patrick stood hesitating, flushing uncomfortably. "I— I'm afraid I don't know the look of the things you mean, sir. What was it you called them?"

The chandler snapped his fingers with the air of a man who has stupidly forgotten a thing he should have remembered. "To be sure," he exclaimed, "thee wouldn't. What thee must look for is a couple of short iron chains with heavy hooks on both ends." A twinkle came into his eyes. " 'Twas trammels I asked for. But I might have called for gib-crokes or potrakes or hangles or deps. Articles of the like have sundry names and a chandler must learn to recognize them by any."

Patrick made a droll face. " 'Twill be luck do I recognize them at all," he laughed. But he hurried off to the barn and returned presently carrying two stout chains answering the chandler's description.

"Fine," said Joshua, taking them from him. "Now thee knows trammels for all time." He held one of the chains up for the boy to observe. "Can thee guess what purpose they serve, lad?"

Patrick recalled his reference to hanging the pots and hazarded a guess. "I'd imagine they're used to suspend kettles above a fire, sir."

"Exactly," replied the chandler. He slipped the top hooks of both chains over the lug pole and hung two of the kettles on the hooks at their lower ends. "There!" he announced. "Now we're ready for work."

By that time Jonathan had returned with firewood and began laying a carefully arranged fire. Before he finished Hannah came running out carrying a long-handled shovel upon which a heap of embers from the kitchen fireplace were smoldering. The boy took it, slipped the coals off beneath the logs and soon the fire was burning with a clear, steady flame.

Then the chandler told the two boys to bring the hampers of berries from the barn, and by the time the last one was set a few feet from the fire Naomi had arrived laden with a pile of flat-bottomed baskets and an assortment of gourd dippers, long-handled stirring paddles, and big wooden ladles. When the kettles began to steam, Joshua and Hannah each took a dipper and began ladling berries into the pots.

Patrick thought he knew what was going to happen. "Oh," he remarked in some surprise, "you have to cook them first!"

Joshua cast him one of his most whimsical smiles. "In a manner of speaking," he replied noncommittally. Then, taking two of the stirring paddles from Naomi, he handed one to Patrick and began stirring the berries in one of the kettles with the other. "Do thee stir the other kettle, lad, in the same manner—gently, round and round, thus."

He illustrated painstakingly and Patrick imitated as nearly as he could. In a few minutes he noticed rings of an oily substance beginning to appear on the surface of the water. He remarked on the fact to Joshua and added, laughing, "It looks for all the world like a soup kettle in which a piece of good fat meat is stewing."

The chandler paused in his stirring and looked at the boy, his eyes narrowed with interest and with some idea that had just come to him. "Ah," he exclaimed in a pleased tone, "so thee has noted a soup kettle then? And did thee perchance see the same kettle when the soup was cold?"

For a moment Patrick couldn't remember. "I think I must have," he replied doubtfully, staring at the oil-ringed water and thinking hard. Suddenly the remembrance came. "To be sure I did," he cried. "The fat had all got hard and formed a solid white cake over near the whole top of the kettle."

Joshua gave a satisfied nod. "Just so," he answered. "The

same thing happens with our berries. The wax, being but an outside coating, is easily melted off by the boiling water and rises to the top just like the fat in the soup kettle. Likewise it cakes just the same when it cools. When 'tis thoroughly cold, a cake of wax near a half inch thick will be floating on the surface of the water and can be lifted off all in one piece."

A droll expression of blank, questioning surprise appeared on Patrick's face. "And is that *all* you do to get the wax?" he demanded.

"That's all," replied Joshua, and it was evident he was trying not to laugh.

The others were not so considerate. Jonathan gave vent to a hilarious whoop. Naomi added her warm, good-natured chuckle, and even Hannah contributed a little ripple of amusement.

Patrick looked around at them with a sheepish grin. "As simple as that," he remarked in a flat tone. "And here I was expecting to see some lengthy and troublesome process."

His chagrin was so evident that Hannah stopped laughing at once and hastened to reassure him. "In a way thee was right, too, Patrick. Getting the wax from the berries *is* simple, but there is a lot more to do ere it can be used for candles. The crude wax has to be refined and that task is indeed a lengthy and troublesome one—just as thee said."

The boy glanced quickly at Joshua for corroboration of the girl's words, fearing Hannah was only trying to make him feel less foolish.

The chandler answered his look with a kindly smile. "That's a fact, lad. Refining bayberry wax takes more skill and patience than aught else a chandler has to do."

It made Patrick feel better someway to know that all of preparing bayberry wax was not so simple, and he returned contentedly to his stirring. Before long the oily substance covered the entire surface of the water, and when he put his paddle down through it and then drew it out carefully he noted the oil mark was indeed half an inch deep upon it.

He turned to announce the fact and saw that Joshua was just lifting his kettle from its hook. "I thought 'twould be ready now," answered the chandler. "Take it off and bring it over to the water-trough to set to cool." He led the way to a wooden trough filled with water which stood in a cool, shady spot close to the barn. "Setting the kettles in cold water makes them cool so much faster that this wax will be hard by the time we've the other four kettles boiled," he explained.

When they returned to the fire, more berries were put into two of the other kettles; they took the places of the first pair and the careful stirring was resumed. When, in turn, those had been boiled enough, they joined the first pair in the trough and the third two were filled and hung to boil.

By the time those were ready to come off the lug pole, the wax in the first kettles was formed into thick cakes on top of the water just as Joshua had said it would be. The chandler took a knife and deftly passed it round the kettles' rim to loosen the wax, then lifted out the round, solid cakes, shook them free of water and laid them aside in one of the round flat-bottomed baskets which exactly fitted the cakes.

Then the kettles were emptied of water and of the worthless berries, refilled and returned to the fire—and the process began all over again.

So it went all day. The stirring had to be kept up constantly and all the family took turns at it, relieving each other at intervals since after a time it became a hot and exhausting task. Before the day was over Patrick's arm was lame and he felt an aching weariness which reminded him unhappily of the deadly fatigue of those last days before he had taken refuge in the chandler's house.

It was past sundown by the time the wax had been removed from all the berries. Jonathan put out the fire, the empty hampers were returned to the barn and, while Hannah was removing the last of the hardened wax from the kettles, Joshua and Naomi gathered up all the things that had been brought out from the house.

"We'll come back later for the wax," Joshua announced. Then, turning to Patrick, he added, "Thee had best stay and help Hannah with bringing in the first load."

Patrick went over to the girl and found her standing with one of the cakes of wax in her hand, gazing down at it with a strange expression of thoughtful wonder on her face. She felt him beside her and looked up at him with shining eyes. "I was thinking about the wax, Patrick," she told him. "I can ne'er get over thinking what a marvel it is that we can get it so from little berries we gather on our own hills." She gave a constrained little laugh. " 'Tis strange I ne'er get used to the idea of it. Each year it seems just as much a marvel to me as it did the first time I saw it."

Bayberries, their wax, and the whole business of obtaining it had become so thoroughly wearisome to Patrick by that time that the girl's wondering enthusiasm awakened nothing in him but an irritated impatience. He picked up a piece of the wax and stood turning it about in his hands. "I see naught so marvelous about it," he remarked with a shrug.

The wax was a dull, dark green, mottled with dingy, gray-green streaks of dirt and flecked with darker spots where bits of stems and leaves had hardened in it. Its dingy green color and the greasy look of its begrimed surface were peculiarly repulsive to him someway. He stared at it with puckered brows wondering why it should stir such unpleasant feelings in him. The next moment he knew. It reminded him of the dirty, oil-smeared, refuse-laden water lapping about the docks in Belfast where he had been kidnapped!

That remembrance awakened a train of other painful memories and, in his weariness, he linked them all with the wax. A wave of loathing for it swept over him. He threw the cake he had picked up back into the basket. " 'Tis beyond me how you can see aught that's marvelous in a thing so ugly," he said harshly.

Hannah stared at him in startled incredulity as though she could not believe her ears that anyone could speak so of the wax. She stood silent for a moment, then her eyes went questioningly to the cake in her hand and rested unhappily upon it as though she were seeing it as it really was for the first time. "Thee is right, I suppose," she admitted at length in a voice filled with puzzled hurt, "but somehow I ne'er seem to see the wax as it looks in this stage. I see it with my mind's eye as it will look when the refining's done."

The unhappiness on her face and the sound of hurt in her voice brought a quick cry of contrition from the boy. "Forgive me, Hannah," he begged. "The wax put me so

106

much in mind of ugly things I have seen."

She looked up at him again, smiling her pardon. But the expression with which she had been looking at the wax still lingered in her eyes. It was a strange look of far-seeing. It gave Patrick an uncanny feeling that she was looking at him and through him and beyond him all at the same time and that she was not seeing him as he was now but as he would be sometime in the future—just as she saw the wax, not as it was now but as it would be when it was refined. He could not understand it, but a kind of certainty came over him that she really could see people and things that way—as they would be sometime.

"I—I know, Hannah," he faltered. "You—you would see it like that."

She did not answer in words; but her eyes thanked him. Then as she stood looking at him a light of deep and radiant gladness came into them.

"What was it made her look so glad," the boy wondered later as they were walking toward the house side by side, each carrying a pile of wax-filled baskets. Then suddenly it didn't matter—for he was glad too. The bitter load of the unhappy past seemed to have fallen from his heart. He felt clear and light and unclouded. "Why," he thought happily, "mayhap 'twas like that she was seeing me."

8

BAYBERRY DIPS AND TALLOW MOLDS

PATRICK had taken for granted the work of refining would be done at the outdoor fire in the barnyard also. So the next morning as soon as he had finished his early meal he proposed eagerly that he should go out and get it started.

The chandler turned a look of shocked surprise upon him. "Mercy, boy, refining can't be done in the open. Dust would blow back into the wax faster than we could skim it out. We work indoors at the bench for that." Then, noting how crestfallen the boy looked at having made such an error, he added hastily, "But there's a chore of fire building thee can do none-the-less." He crossed to his bench and drew out a brazier and a box of charcoal from beneath it. "For refining we use charcoal heat," he explained, "because it makes neither smoke nor ashes to further foul the wax."

Patrick's face broke into smiles of happy recognition. "Oh," he exclaimed, "I know about charcoal. 'Tis much used at home. I can start the brazier easily."

He took it to the hearth and filled the bottom with live coals from the fireplace; then lump by lump he laid in the charcoal and, taking the bellows, blew gently on them until they were all aglow.

108

While he was working he noticed that Joshua was taking down a number of shallow iron kettles and an assortment of strainers and long-handled skimmers from the shelves above his bench and setting them out upon it in orderly array.

The baskets containing the wax had all been stacked beneath the bench the night before, and when Patrick brought the lighted brazier over the chandler asked him to pile some of them on the bench itself so they would be conveniently at hand for melting. When that was done he told him cheerily, "Now draw up stools for thyself and Hannah. Only we three will be working because my good wife refuses to have any hand in this bothersome task and Jonathan is yet too young to have patience sufficient for it."

Before Patrick had been long at work he decided Mistress Mapes had showed herself a canny woman by refusing to take part in it, and soon he even began to wonder if he, himself, were much better fitted for it than Jonathan. For never in his life had he attempted anything that tried him so sorely.

Enough of the wax was melted to fill three of the shallow kettles with the smoking, sweet-smelling liquid. This was strained and kept in a liquid state by frequent reheating and, as the impurities which could not be strained out rose to the surface, they were skimmed off with infinite care. Nothing short of unwavering attention and unlimited patience would accomplish the desired results.

It took several days to finish all the wax, and there were many times during those days when Patrick was seized with such furious impatience he wanted to hurl the kettle into the farthest corner of the room and rush out of the house away from the pervading scent of bayberry.

Nothing of the kind ever happened, however, for usually at such times Joshua would note his state and send him off on some outdoor errand. So he managed to endure the work and the day came, at length, when all the baskets which had once contained the ugly, dull green cakes were filled instead with wax of a pure and lovely soft green color.

Patrick could not get over his surprise at the transformation, and remarked upon it as they were piling away the finished cakes. "It seems beyond believing that a thing so ugly could be made so fair," he said.

Hannah gave him a happy smile. "Thee can understand better now why I feel as I do, can't thee, Patrick?" she asked.

"I understood before—really," he assured her, "but I know why now that I have seen the thing happen." He recalled the memories the appearance of the crude wax had stirred in him and gave a heavy sigh. "I only wish 'twere as easy to refine away the ugly things the crude wax made me think about."

The girl stood looking at him thoughtfully a long moment. "Perchance it is," she said in a low voice at length. "But we don't know the way to do it—nor believe it could be done. Were we that way about the wax, 'twould still be the same ugly stuff thee disliked so much."

Patrick made no reply. Something deep within himself told him the girl was right. Yet, with his mind, he could not see how she could be. So he only shrugged and turned back to work again.

The next task to be undertaken was a similar preparation of the fats stored in the cellar. The casks were brought up and the boys rolled them out to the barnyard. The fire there was started again, the fat was ladled into two great kettles, tried out, and then as it was reduced to a liquid dipped off into smaller kettles and set aside to cool. In a few hours it was hardened into cakes the same as the bayberry wax except that the tallow was a dingy cream color.

These were brought into the house and later were refined much as the bayberry wax had been, and when the cakes were hard again they were a pure, clear ivory ready for molding into the finest tallow candles.

By that time the better part of two weeks had gone by and Patrick was beginning to feel they were never going to reach the place where they would actually begin to make candles. He voiced his feeling to Hannah and she nodded with sympathetic understanding.

"I know just how thee feels," she told him, "for I have many, many times felt the same myself. When folk must prepare all the stuff for candle making themselves, it cannot help but take a sight of time. But now as soon as we've filled a dipping of candle rods we can start on the dips."

She went to the shelves above the work-bench and began taking down several bundles of smooth wooden rods which she handed to Patrick. They were about a foot and a half long, as big around as a candle and were polished to a satin smoothness. He recalled that during the first day of his instruction Hannah had told him the reason loops were left open at the top of the twisted wicks was so a rod could be run through them to hold them for dipping. Therefore he was not entirely at sea as to the use of the odd sticks.

"Put them on the table with the wicks," she commanded, "and then thee can get down the poles for me."

She pointed out two poles, nearly eight feet long, stretched on the rafters, and standing on one of the stools from the table the boy took them down and handed them to her.

"Some rest the ends of the poles on stools," she said as she took them, "but we have racks made specially to hold them. They are there in the far corner." And she pointed to a pair of wooden rests which Patrick had supposed were trestles for some unusually narrow table-board.

He drew them forth from the corner and turned to the girl to ask where he was to put them.

"There in the far end of the room where they are," she replied. "They must be as far from the fireplace as can be, so the candles may harden."

Patrick set them as far apart as he estimated the length of the poles to be, then took the poles from Hannah.

"Thee will find grooves in the racks where the poles should rest," she told him. "Father put them there so there'd be no danger they'd be jarred off and let the candles fall."

"The poles have grooves in them too," Patrick remarked, indicating a series of evenly spaced depressions along the entire length of both poles. "Those must be to rest the rods in."

Hannah flashed him a pleased smile. "Aye, they are," she answered. "It makes dipping go faster when there's a place provided to set the rods into so there's no chance of their slipping. Now," she added, turning back to the other side of the room, "we'll set the wax to melt and then we can fix the wicks. Do thee get out the kettle while I fetch the wax."

Patrick got the kettle and set it on the hearth and Han-

nah brought one of the baskets of bayberry wax and laid
a cake within it.

"These first candles will be pure bayberry wax because
they are our traveler's candles and we ne'er make them any
other way—and 'tis my notion we should always do them
first."

What she had said suggested to the boy that all the
candles were not to be pure bayberry and he asked the
question.

"Nay," replied Hannah, "only a small part, for they are
the most costly and few will pay the price for pure bayberry. For the others we mix bayberry wax and tallow in
different amounts. The price of the candle varies with the
amount of bayberry. A fourth of bayberry even makes a
fragrant candle."

When they took their places at the table where the wicks
lay waiting, she pointed to a pile of wicks longer than the
others. "Those are the ones we are to fix now," she said.
"They are for the traveler's candles because we make them
longer than ordinary candles." She picked up a rod and
began running it rapidly through the loops of the twisted
wicks. "Put eight wicks on each rod, spaced evenly and
far enough apart so the candles will not touch each other
e'en do they swing a bit."

Patrick set industriously to work and soon all the rods
were filled. Hannah took enough of them to fill all the
grooves on the poles and fitted them into the grooves so
they stretched from pole to pole with their wicks dangling limply. Then she went back to the fireplace, glanced
in the kettle, and announced the wax was melted.

"Lift one of the kettles of boiling water off the lug pole
for me, now, will thee please, Patrick?" she asked.

The boy looked at her in surprise. "Water!" he exclaimed. "What has that to do with candle making?"

Hannah smiled at him mysteriously. "Lift it off and thee will see."

So Patrick lifted the kettle from its trammel and set it on the hearth.

"We pour the melted wax in on top of it thus," she said, suiting the action to the words. "Thee sees what happens. The wax stays floating on top of the water. The heat under it serves to keep it liquid longer and the fact that it is supported toward the top of the kettle makes dipping easier." She dropped another cake of wax into the melting kettle so it would be ready when the other was used up and turned to Patrick with one of her beaming smiles. "So now, at long last, we are ready to dip. Take the dipping kettle over by the poles and we will start."

When it was set conveniently near, she took the first of the rods from its resting place and lowered the wicks gently into the wax up to where the loops began. Then she replaced it on the pole, took the second, and dipped it in the same way. When she had replaced that, she pointed to the first rod and said, "Strip the wicks on that quickly ere the wax gets too hard, while I do the second lot. Watch, I will show thee."

She took hold of the bottom of a limply dangling wick and pulled it down straight. Then, using the thumb and first finger of the other hand, she grasped it just below the loop and drew firmly downward a number of times until the wax was hard and the wick hung firm and straight. "See," she said, holding up the rod, "the wick now forms a perfect base for a candle."

Patrick caught the idea and rapidly did the rest. Then

114

they dipped the other rods and stripped them in the same manner. When they were all done the poles looked as though they had rows and rows of tiny icicles hanging from them.

"Candles are built up slowly, layer by layer, by repeated dipping," Hannah explained. "When two are working together they must adopt a rhythm. I dip; then as I hang my rod, thee dips. Then as thee hangs thine, I dip again, and so we go on through the length of the poles. By the time we have reached the last rod, the first is hard enough for another dipping and we start all over again."

That was the way it was done and layer by layer the candles grew. When the floating wax was all used up, a second kettle hanging over the fire was prepared and the first returned to the lug pole for the water to get hot again. Then when the second was exhausted, the first was ready to use again. Thus they alternated and gradually the candles grew until they were full-formed. By evening they had finished three hundred and sixty-five fat green candles —a traveler's candle for every night in the year.

The next morning the chandler asked Naomi if she would help Hannah with the dipping so that Patrick could work with him at the bench. "I'd like to have him get the hang of using the molds so he can keep the tallow candles going along with the dips."

Patrick was anxious to learn all there was to know about making candles as rapidly as possible, so he greeted the suggestion eagerly.

" 'Twill really be simple for thee," Joshua began, "as no doubt thee has oft seen candles molded at home. But a chandler's way differs somewhat from the housewife's method."

Patrick gave an embarrassed little laugh. "I must confess, sir, that I've ne'er seen candles made at all. I ne'er thought to question where those we used so freely came from. They were not made in the house, of that I am sure."

Joshua chuckled. "So? Then some chandler made a pretty penny on thy father's trade. Well, since thee knows naught of the business, we had best begin at the beginning." He reached up to one of the shelves above the bench and took down a small pewter mold designed to fashion six candles at a time. "This is a housewife's mold," he said, holding it up for Patrick to see.

Then he set it down and drew forward one of the great molds standing along the back of the bench. Evidently it was made to turn out two dozen candles at a time, for it consisted of two long rows of twelve cylinders mounted in a heavy wooden frame. The bottom of each cylinder terminated in a point. Two light metal rods the length of the row were supported above the open tops of the cylinders by means of notches in the wooden frame.

"And this," he went on, "is a chandler's mold. Note the difference. The chandler's mold turns out four times as many candles at a molding. It is provisioned with a rod across the top upon which the wicks may be suspended in the cylinders while the housewife must contrive some way of hanging wicks on bits of wire or the like laid across the top of the openings. Then when the candles are hard there is no way for a housewife to get them out of the mold except to plunge the mold into hot water so a bit of the outside of the tallow is melted and the candles will slip out. But in the chandler's mold an entire row may be lifted out at once by means of the rod."

He lifted one of the rods from its resting place to illustrate and, when he had returned it, showed Patrick the pointed bottoms of the cylinders. "Thee sees, too, that when the candles come from a chandler's mold they are all neatly pointed at the top, while those from a housewife's mold are alike at both ends and must be heated at one end and shaped to a point with the fingers."

He set the small mold back upon the shelf and continued. "So thee can readily see that molding candles a chandler's way is much more handy than the housewife's as well as turning out a far more perfect candle. But there is one chore a chandler has to do that a housewife does not. Before the stuff for the candles can be poured into these great molds, they must have the wicks threaded in—and that is a little task in itself." He gave the boy a cheery smile. "That is what I want thee to learn to do now. Pass me a handful of wicks and I will show thee."

Patrick did so and Joshua laid the pile between them on the bench. "First off they must all be knotted at the end opposite the loop to keep them from pulling through when they are drawn into the mold. Do thee do half and I will do the rest."

They fell to work and in no time the wicks in the pile were all neatly knotted.

While he was working, the boy had been casting a speculative eye over the mold and when the wicks were finished he asked, "May I try threading one before you tell me, sir? I think I've figured how 'tis done."

The chandler agreed heartily and pushed the mold over to the boy. He turned the frame over on its side and saw that, just as he had surmised, there was a hole in the pointed end of each cylinder. "You run the loop end of the wick in through that hole, don't you, sir? Then pull it up to the top so the rod can be run through the loop?"

"Exactly," replied Joshua in a pleased tone. "Now go ahead with it." He handed the boy a small wire instrument with a hook at the end. "This will help thee in drawing them to the top," he said.

Patrick gave himself to the task with interest and in a few minutes the wicks of one row were in and the rod run through their loops.

"Note how firm and true the wicks are held," said Joshua. "Now when the candles are ready to be taken out, all we have to do is snip off the knots and out they come." He nodded to the row of molds along the back of the bench. "Half of them are threaded. We'll do the balance now, then pour in the melted tallow and let them stand till the morrow. After the candles are taken out they have to be trimmed smooth on the bottoms—and then they are ready for market." He smiled genially at the boy. "Thee will find it all a simple task, I'm sure."

Patrick did find it all simple. In a few days he could thread the molds as dexterously as the chandler, pour the liquid tallow with as steady a hand, and trim the bottoms of the finished candles true with one stroke of the knife kept sharp for the purpose.

Days slipped rapidly by. Sometimes he worked at the bench with Joshua, sometimes he dipped with Hannah, and sometimes he worked with Jonathan packing the finished candles in home-made boxes of hand-riven wood, separating them carefully according to kind.

Most of the days were mild and sunny and the shutters at the window holes stood open. But on two there was cold rain again, and when the shutters were closed Naomi fretted gently. Patrick said nothing, but in his heart he sympathized with her for there were times when he found it very hard to adjust himself to the discomforts of the crude little house.

But though his new life was sometimes trying physically, spiritually it gave him peace and healing. Amid the consistent kindness, tolerance, and good will that surrounded him the cruelties, tyranny, and injustices of the Old World seemed almost a bad dream without reality. Yet he had not forgotten his desire to meet Roger Williams and question him about those ideas of his which he held would do away with man's persecution of his fellows. Sometimes as they worked he asked Joshua about them; but the chandler steadfastly refused to be drawn into a presentation of Roger Williams' philosophy. "I'd rather Master Williams expounded those matters to thee himself," he would say. "He can do it so much more ably than I."

But bit by bit he did tell the boy the important facts regarding the remarkable man. How, when but a lad, he had begun to question the authority of the English Church, and how as a young man he had thrown himself into exhaustive study in an effort to justify the ideas unfolding in his mind. At another time he told of his decision to seek a place of greater freedom of thought in America, of his clash with the narrowness of the church of Massachusetts Bay, and of his final banishment.

"But to what faith does he belong then?" asked the boy. "I take it he is no longer Puritan."

"He is now what is termed a 'Seeker,'" answered Joshua, "and the name suits him well. For that is just what he is— an eternal seeker after truth. His first departure from orthodox Puritanism was to become a Separatist like the Pilgrims. Then for a time after coming here he espoused the faith of a group that call themselves Baptists. But no sect can hold him long. His is a mind that must chart its own course." His eyes began to twinkle with some amusing thought and he broke into a series of chuckles. "Because of these changes of view his enemies in the Bay call him 'Master Weathercock' and say that, like that indicator of the winds of heaven, he is consistent only in his inconsistency."

Patrick laughed also. But his laughter held understanding and sympathy rather than derision. "In my view 'tis a sight better to be a weathercock than a church pillar," he declared. "A weathercock does at least catch the breath of Heaven." He went on working in silence a moment, then added, "But to my way of thinking 'tis of no worth for a man to attain freedom of thought for himself unless he accords it to others also—and that is what I doubt he'd do in the end."

"Aye, but he has," answered Joshua quickly, "though to do so has cost him many a battle with others in power in his own Plantation, as well as with the authorities of the other colonies. Such a battle he had about receiving the Friends here, and e'en a worse one when he proposed to admit the persecuted Jews of Spain and Portugal who had sought refuge in America and been refused entrance by the other settlements." He paused to give vent to a dry, meaningful laugh. "And for all the to-do it turned out in the end that now the Friends are held in such esteem that one of our members is the present Governor of the Plantation and 'tis the Jews that settled in Newport who have done most to build the place up into a port near like to Boston."

The remark about the Quaker Governor caught Patrick's attention especially. He had surmised that Roger Williams would still hold that post and said as much.

"He still serves the colony in many ways," replied the chandler, "but he was glad to be relieved of the responsibility of being Governor. After all, the man is now past his seventieth year and his life has been one of constant struggle."

Patrick thought about the things he had heard as he worked. Gradually the bayberry wax and the tallow were transformed into candles, and at last an evening came when the baskets stacked under the bench were empty. The finished candles were all packed in boxes ready for loading on Christopher the next morning so he could carry them to Providence to be sold.

Joshua placed his hands on the boy's shoulders and smiled down at him with affectionate approval. "Thee has done nobly, my boy. I could not have asked a better helper had I searched the country o'er. I trust thee is as content here as we are to have thee."

The words Patrick wanted to say in reply would not come, but the look in his eyes as he stood gazing back into the chandler's face answered the question.

Evidently Joshua was satisfied with that answer for he went on without waiting for another, "So be thee should be, 'tis my plan to start right off to building an addition to the house where we can have a proper shop so we can expand our trade this coming year. Does all go well, thee will have a good trade of thy own in a few years or, did thee prefer, thee could stay here and become my partner."

Patrick found his voice quickly to answer the last

sentence. "Oh, sir," he said eagerly, "an thee would be willing, 'twould please me best to stay and be thy partner."

Joshua glanced quickly at Naomi to see if she had noticed that the boy had slipped unconsciously into the use of their plain speech. Evidently she had. Tears stood in her eyes but her face was shining. She knew that the wandering boy she had taken into her heart belonged to them now in very truth.

9

THE FOUNDER OF PROVIDENCE

JOSHUA pointed to a row of housetops that had just come into view. "Well, Patrick, there's Providence," he announced.

Patrick halted involuntarily in his surprised disappointment. "You—you mean those few houses?" he faltered. He had thought so much about the place that he had built up a vivid mental picture of what it would be like. It would be simple of course, he had imagined, but there would be a sort of grandeur about it as befitted a spot where a great idea was coming into being—a dignity in appearance in some degree equal to its dignity in the destiny of men. It seemed incredible this crude little hamlet made up of a single street running along parallel to an estuary with salt marshes on the opposite shore could really be the Providence of which he had dreamed.

The chandler gave him an apologetic smile. "It looks like naught to thee compared to the great towns to which thee has been accustomed, I venture. But thee must bear in mind 'tis not yet thirty years since its founding."

The boy tugged at Christopher's lead rope and started on again. "To be sure," he agreed with assumed heartiness. "I should have had that in mind. I just thought 'twould look more important someway."

"More elegant, you mean?" asked Hannah, who walked on his other side. "It couldn't well be that because near all the folk who came here were poor in the world's goods."

"Aye," added Joshua. "Many had naught but the land granted them by the colony to start with."

Patrick was beginning to feel very uncomfortable. He wanted nothing so much as to dismiss the matter of his misconception of Providence altogether and seized eagerly upon Joshua's statement as a new topic of discussion. "You mean they were given land free—without paying for it at all?" he asked.

Joshua nodded. "Absolutely. The heads of each family were all granted a parcel of exactly the same size."

They had started down the street by this time and Patrick regarded the homes that lined it with new interest. The houses all stood on the same side of the street facing the estuary and the marsh beyond. They were all set back upon plots of ground of exactly the same shape and size. He estimated there were about thirty houses, and they all looked so much alike it would have been hard to tell one from another. In shape and material they were not unlike the Mapes house, except that they all had leaded glass casements and shingled roofs in place of thatch.

It had been decided that they should pay their visit to Roger Williams before they started on the work of disposing of their candles in order to be more sure of catching him before he left his house in pursuit of one of his many activities. So when they were about halfway down the street, Joshua stopped. "This is Master Williams' house," he announced. "Get his candles off the pack and we will take them in as we go."

Each year Joshua prepared a box of his finest candles

for his benefactor in grateful remembrance of the sanctuary he had been given in the colony. The box in which they had been packed with special care topped one of the piles stacked in hanging crates suspended from Christopher's packsaddle.

Patrick started to untie the thongs that held the box in place and while he was doing so the door opened and a man came eagerly out to greet them. It was plain he was no longer young, for the hair that blew back from his high forehead was white as snow. But his step was still quick and his body showed the vigor of a man who has spent much of his life in rugged outdoor pursuits.

"Greetings and welcome, Friend Mapes," he called heartily, advancing to meet Joshua with hand extended. "I've been looking for you these many days."

The two men shook hands warmly, Roger Williams gave Hannah a kiss on the brow, and then turned to look questioningly at Patrick.

"And who is this fine lad?" he asked. "I've ne'er seen him with you ere this."

Joshua laid his arm about Patrick's shoulders. "Nay, thee has not for he came to me not a month since. His name is Patrick. He has proved himself so fine a helper we hope one day he may become my partner. He has but lately come from the Old World where he has seen much of its strife. He has heard of what is being done here so he's been burning for a chance to meet thee."

"He has?" said Roger Williams with interest. Then turning to the boy he added, "And why is that, Patrick?"

Patrick was covered with confusion and hardly knew what to say. "I—I had heard of your ideas, sir, and I wanted to hear you tell about them."

Roger Williams' expression was a mixture of pleasure and mild surprise. "You don't say!" he exclaimed. "A lad of your age! Well, come in, come in. The wind is sharp this morning. We can talk of all these matters beside the fire."

He started back to the house chatting volubly with Joshua. Patrick did not follow at once as he was still busied getting the candles from the pack and, when that was done, in tying Christopher to the hitching post beside the gate. Hannah remained with him and the two men had already established themselves by the fire before they came in.

Roger Williams sat in a big armchair on one side of the hearth and Joshua on the settle opposite. As they entered, their host made apologies for not having waited for them.

"My old bones feel the bite of the cold these days," he laughed. "Put the candles down, my boy, and come over by the fire." He nodded invitingly to a low stool at his feet. "Come sit here beside me, Hannah child," he begged, smiling on the girl with evident affection. "I miss having little girls about me sorely since all my own are women grown and gone."

Hannah settled herself beside his knees and Patrick perched on the settle beside Joshua. Then the two men plunged back into discussion of the affairs of the colony.

Patrick was glad to be ignored and have a chance to observe this man of whom he had heard so much. His face was a strange mixture. His fine well-domed forehead bespoke the thoughtful student; his piercing eyes the far-seeing idealist; a jutting nose, rugged cheekbones, and square set jaw the indomitable crusader. But his mouth and chin were those of a man whose affections were warm

and played an important part in his life. There was a sort
of headlong impetuosity about him. His speech poured
from him as though he could hardly wait to unburden an
over-crowded mind. He veered from one topic to another
with such suddenness it was difficult to keep abreast of his
thought.

"Master Weathercock," thought Patrick with an in-
ward smile. "It suits him sure enough, but for all that I'm
mortal certain that once he set his mind naught could
change him."

The thing the boy had feared most was that he would
detect signs of insincerity in the man. Now he dismissed
that idea once and for all. "He might misjudge a thing,"
he thought, "because he'd have his heart so set on having
it the way he saw it, but he could ne'er make pretense of
a thing he did not feel."

Having come to those important conclusions he could
relax and look about the room. It was evidently not used
as general living quarters but as a study. There were no
signs of domesticity about it, but it was filled with evidences that it was used by one who followed the writer's
craft. A big writing table bearing ink pot, sand box, an
assortment of quill pens, and piles of manuscript stood
beneath the window; shelves filled with books lined the
walls on each side of the fireplace; more books were piled
on a small candle-stand at their host's elbow, and stray
volumes and sheaves of papers littered every available resting place.

Patrick had seen no books since leaving home and his
eyes devoured them hungrily. He was so absorbed trying
to make out the titles he did not notice the turn the talk
had taken until he heard Joshua speak Paucottauwat's

name. That brought his attention back to what was being said, and he found that the chandler was recounting their strange interview with the Indian.

"It had ne'er occurred to me that Metacomet's resentment toward us might have grown from the fact that we were alienating his tribesmen from their own faith," he was saying.

Roger Williams made a gesture of impatient surprise. "And why not, my friend?" he demanded. " 'Tis entirely logical. A man's heart is where his faith is. Metacomet knows all too well that those of his people that are converted to the white man's faith are lost to their own race. He said as much to me once. He said he was soon like to be a king without a people. He would fight against that sooner than to regain the lands he has so unwisely bartered." He shook his head with a sigh. "Aye, 'twas a bitter error to tamper with the red man's faith."

Patrick spoke before he could stop himself. "But I thought you were a missionary to the Indians once yourself, sir."

His host showed no resentment but turned to him with a smile in which kindness and regret mingled. "I sought to be when I first came here to America, a young man filled with zeal. But ere long I saw my error. And 'twas really Metacomet's father, Massasoit, who showed it to me. We had become fast friends. He held me especially dear because I had made the stand that the American lands belonged to the Indians instead of to the king of England as the English claimed, and that we could only obtain them legally by purchase from their native owners. That idea of mine was one of the things over which I came to such outs with the Bay Colony." With that he veered off to a recital of some of his other difficulties with Massachusetts and Patrick was forced to bring him back to the first topic.

"But about Massasoit," the boy reminded him. "What was it he did to make you see your error?"

His host gave a good-natured laugh. "Ah, to be sure. I got off that, didn't I?" He paused and seemed to rein in his headlong thoughts. "When missionary efforts first commenced among the Indians," he began again, "the old Chief had petitioned that the religion of his people should not be interfered with. No attention was paid to his plea and he did naught because he held his white friends too dear. But when we talked together and I spoke of my dream of a world where each man should have full right to his own faith, he would demand to know why then did I not feel the Indian had an equal right to his. I could not but see that he was right. So when I came here among the Narragansetts, I made it one of the laws of the Plantation that the Indians' faith should be accorded the same tolerance and respect as that we pledged ourselves to extend to white men of varying beliefs who came to settle amongst us."

The sentence upon which he had ended made a perfect opening for the question Patrick had so much wanted to ask and he put it quickly before his host could be off on another topic. "But is it possible to get men to do that, sir?" he demanded. "I mean respect each other's beliefs as you said. I have seen so much cruelty and hate because of different faiths in Ireland where I lived that I have doubted men could be changed."

Roger Williams looked at him with sharp interest. "So you come from that hot-bed of strife, eh? And to which camp did you belong?"

Patrick outlined his backgrounds briefly while the older man listened with grave respect. When the boy ceased speaking, he sat looking at him in silence a moment, an expression of deep sorrow on his face. "How pitiful that such a thing should be," he said at length with a deep sigh, "when the cure is in truth so easy." He leaned forward in his chair speaking with great earnestness. "You can see easily, can you not, lad, that such a sad state comes about only because rulers have power to dictate about matters that should by right be only the affair of the man they concern? There is only one law valid when it comes to religion. That is the law of the spirit. The law of the land has naught to do with that—and should not be allowed to have."

"Aye, sir," replied Patrick in a puzzled tone, "I can see that without trouble. But how could it be otherwise? Rulers do as they will and the people must bow to their wishes or pay the price for refusing to do so."

Roger Williams made an eager gesture. "That's as it is now. But government should be organized the other way round. The people should be the ones to dictate. A ruler should be only a servant of the people. They it is who should make the laws and grant a ruler of their choice the power and commission to have them executed."

Patrick's face was blank with amazement. He had never heard of such an idea in all his life. At first it was almost impossible for him to grasp its significance, but gradually its magnitude and magnificence began to dawn upon him. He was so overcome by the picture it presented he could hardly speak. "Why," he breathed barely above a whisper, "so be such a thing could come to pass, 'twould make the world a different place. Every man would have a chance instead of just a few. There—there would really be such a thing as freedom."

The faces of the two older men were soft with sympathetic feeling. Joshua laid his hand on the boy's knee with a gesture of comradeship and understanding.

"Thee did not say so specifically just now," he said to Roger Williams, "but I take it this new sort of government of which thee speaks would have no state church, nor a hand in religious matters at all. Each man would be free to think and worship as he saw fit." It was plain he was trying to make sure the boy grasped that important fact.

Williams gave an emphatic nod. "Absolutely. I thought I made that plain a while back."

Patrick was still quite dazed. "Then there'd be no reason for men to hate each other," he said incredulously.

Joshua patted his knee. "That's right, son," he told him gently.

The boy sat silent awhile thinking, and gradually the look of wonder passed from his face and in its place came an expression of bitter doubt. "Why talk about it?" he said finally with a shrug. " 'Twould be impossible for such a thing to happen. Men would not accept it."

Roger Williams sat forward in his chair, his eyes gleaming with prophetic light. "They will—in time, as sure as we sit here. I shall not see it except in a small way here in my own colony. None of us here will, perchance. But your children may, lad, and their children will, of that I'm mortal certain."

Patrick did not answer and his face was still filled with troubled question.

"Look what we have accomplished here," his host went on. "We have had gusts among us from time to time, 'tis true. But I have managed to keep our ideals unblemished. So now we have a colony where folk of many diverse faiths are all living together in peace and tolerance."

"And what has been done in a small way," added Joshua eagerly, "can surely be done in a large."

Roger Williams cast him a glance of warm affection. "That is true, my friend. In a way this Plantation has been a holy experiment. We have proved the thing can be done. Little Rhode Island is a light set upon a hill for doubting souls to see."

10

"BETTER CANDLES JUST AS CHEAP"

PATRICK was still in a daze when he left the house of Roger Williams. He started to untie Christopher's hitching rope and fell thinking with the knot half undone and his eyes staring off at nothing.

Joshua watched him with a tenderly indulgent smile for a moment, then, as though loath to break in upon his thoughts, touched him softly on the arm and said in a gentle voice, "Come, lad, there'll be time to ponder all these things when our work is done. We must make haste with our candles now do we hope to finish and get home by sundown."

The boy started out of his reverie and resumed untying the knot.

The chandler put his hand over it with a kindly laugh. "Nay, lad, leave Christopher tied here for the present. The house of Master Throckmorton, whose boxes of candles I had thee put beneath those for Master Williams, is just next door. We may as well unload them here."

"Oh, I remember now," said Patrick, starting to unload the boxes with reassuring briskness. "He is the gentleman who is clerk of the court or some such thing and buys candles for the town as well as his own. So his lot was the most sizable of all."

"Right," answered Joshua. "Give me half the boxes and thee and Hannah can bring the rest."

Their knock brought Mistress Throckmorton to the door. When she saw them on the doorstep with their boxes she did not give them the cordial good morning Patrick expected. Instead an expression of mingled distress and embarrassment came into her face. "Oh, 'tis you, Master Mapes," she said. "Will you put your boxes down outside there and come in a moment? My husband wishes some speech with you."

"Why, surely," replied the chandler in a puzzled tone, setting down his candles and motioning the others to do the same.

Just inside the door they encountered the master of the house who was evidently on his way out to meet them. The two men shook hands, Joshua presented Patrick, and then there was an awkward pause.

"Thy good wife said thee wished some speech with me," said Joshua finally.

Master Throckmorton cleared his throat. "Aye, I did," he answered. " 'Tis about the candles." He paused as though finding it difficult to say what he had planned. "The truth is," he went on at length, "we are supplied for the year."

"Supplied!" echoed Joshua. He stood still an instant gazing at the other man with shocked surprise, then seeming to gather himself together, inquired, "Is there then another chandler in Providence now?"

Master Throckmorton shook his head. "Not in Providence. These come from Newport. It chanced I was there a few weeks since on Plantation business and everywhere

I went I found folk using candles of such brilliance I was fair amazed. When I asked about them I found they were made by some of the Jewish immigrants who had settled in the town some years back. 'Twas my thought that such sovereign candles would be costly, but I discovered their price was the same as for those we get from you. And I tell you honestly, though they are just as cheap, their light is easily twice as bright." He spread his hands outward with a shrug of resigned acceptance. "You see my situation. One of these candles will serve where we use two of yours and so cut the town's outlay for candles just in half. So 'twas plainly my duty to the colony to provision us with those instead."

Joshua heard him out with courteous calm. As far as Patrick could see, he was not in the least shaken by this news which, inexperienced as he was, the boy saw must necessarily mean a serious threat to his means of livelihood. He glanced quickly at Hannah to see if she too sensed the fact. She was standing looking up at Master Throckmorton with quiet, polite attention; but there was a puzzled pucker between her smooth brows as though she were trying to grasp the meaning of what he had said and found it incomprehensible.

"I understand thy position entirely." Joshua's tone was reassuring and soothing as if his concern were all for the other man's discomfort instead of his own loss. He paused a moment, then went on in an impersonal manner, " 'Tis of great interest to one who plies the chandler's trade to hear report of such an advance in candle making. Might I be permitted to see one of these remarkable new candles?"

"Assuredly," replied the other. He stepped to the mantel, and reaching into the candle box above it took two candles from it and handed one to the chandler and the other to Patrick.

The boy fell to examining his with great interest. It was pure white instead of soft ivory. Its surface was smoother and more glossy, and when he tried to scrape off a bit of the substance from which it was made, he found it hard and brittle instead of waxy.

The chandler seemed to need but one glance to know all about the candle. " 'Tis as I thought," he said. "They are made of spermaceti, are they not?"

Master Throckmorton shot a glance of shrewd approval at him. "I see you are not behind the times in knowledge at least, Master Mapes. You're right. They're made of spermaceti."

"Spermaceti?" repeated Hannah in a bewildered tone. "What is that, Father?"

" 'Tis a wax-like substance obtained from the head of the great sperm whale," Joshua answered. "For years chandlers have known that, could some way be devised to render it into a state that could be molded, 'twould make candles far superior to either wax or tallow. But none had been discovered, so far as I knew. Evidently it has been now." He handed back the candle with a wry smile. "The method might be common knowledge and I'd not know of it—we are so cut off from things here."

"Nay, but 'tis not common knowledge," answered the other quickly. "The process is known only to these Jews. 'Tis a trade secret they brought from their homeland." *

* Some liberty has possibly been taken with the dating of the be-ginnings of the great spermaceti industry in New England. Historians attribute the introduction of spermaceti candles to Jacob Rodriquez

Joshua gave a rueful shrug. "In that case we other chandlers are in a sorry plight. What are we to do in such a pass?"

"I've been thinking of that, Friend Mapes," the other man replied in a tone of friendly concern. "You are a man we all respect. Yet none will buy a thing when they can get a better at the same price. Why not give up the trade of chandler? You have education, and since the Quakers are now in power in the Plantation there must be various posts you could be fitted into."

Patrick heard Hannah give a little gasp of protest, but she was too well trained to break into the talk.

Joshua took the candle Patrick was holding and handed it back to their host. " 'Tis kindly of thee to concern thyself about me and I thank thee heartily; but, for the present, I shall try to stick to my trade. Should I find later that I must find another way to earn the bread for my family, I will come to talk over possibilities with thee." He held out his hand in farewell and the two men shook hands as though the interview had been a purely social one.

As soon as they were outside and the door closed, Hannah laid hold of her father's arm. "Thee would ne'er consider giving o'er our candle making, would thee, Father?" she demanded anxiously.

Her father gave her hand a soothing pat. "I think not, daughter," he replied. "I trust things will ne'er come to that pass." He started to gather up the candle boxes he

Rivera who did not join the Jewish settlement in Newport until 1745. However, there seems to be sufficient evidence that spermaceti candles were being made in America by 1670 to justify the assumption that some of Newport's earlier Jewish settlers might have begun making them at the time of our story.

had put down and added cheerfully that they should take the rest. "We'll take them back to the pack, then run into Master Verin's on the other side of Master Williams' house to see how things stand there ere we unload others."

They found the Verin household had also supplied themselves with spermaceti candles for common use. "As you know," Goodwife Verin told the chandler, " 'tis our wont to get a few dozen of the bayberry dips each year in addition to the tallow candles we bought, so we'd have them to burn in a bed-chamber for their cleansing smell in time of sickness or in the best room when we have special guests. Those we will take as always. But I tell you truly, Master Mapes, that once a housewife has cooked a meal or run a seam by the light of these new candles, naught could persuade her to go back to working by the dim light of the old kind again."

So when they went back to where Christopher was tied to get the bayberry dips, the chandler told Patrick to unload the pack and put all the boxes of tallow candles at the bottom of the piles. "Plainly, the way things stand," he said, "so be we are to do any business at all, 'twill be on our bayberry dips."

And events proved he was right. Families that had always used a certain number of dips still bought them. But there were few households that wanted a supply of tallow candles. Usually where they did buy them it was so evident they did so out of friendliness for the chandler that Patrick could see it galled him to accept payment for them.

By the time they had been to half the houses on the street Patrick was thoroughly discouraged. But the chandler gave no sign of distress and chatted cheerfully as they went from house to house.

"We should have good luck here," he said as they turned in to one place. "This is the house of Widow Sears. She has used naught but bayberry dips all her life and I doubt a little thing like a better light from her candles would change her."

Evidently the widow had been watching for them, for before they reached the door she opened it to tell the chandler to bring in her usual number of dips.

They brought in the boxes and as they were stacking them on the shelves she indicated she inquired meaningfully how the chandler was finding business.

"Well," replied Joshua evasively, "I've seen it better."

"I venture you have," the widow remarked pointedly. "Seems like every house I've been in in the last few weeks I've found the folk using these new-fangled candles from Newport."

Joshua admitted he had found many of his usual customers using the Newport candles.

Widow Sears gave a sniff of contempt. "Made by Jews from a foreign land!" There was a world of contempt in her tone. "I call it a shame for Christian folk to do the like when we have a chandler of our own race and kind right here among us."

The chandler gave her a deprecating smile. " 'Tis kind of thee to feel thus for me," he told her mildly, "but I am not complaining, and surely so be I do not thee has no cause to."

"But you should complain," she asserted stoutly. "Such people should not be allowed place in the colony to spoil the trade of honest men of our own kind. When Master Williams came back from England all afire about the state of the persecuted Jewish people and proposed to let them in here, I set myself against it with all my might. But of what use is a woman? They let them come—and now look. I say you should complain and that loudly."

Joshua shook his head. " 'Twould ill become me to do so, Widow Sears, since I am myself one to whom the colony has given sanctuary from persecution." He paused and looked firmly into her eyes. "And in any case I would not do so. This Plantation was founded for those 'distressed for conscience sake.' I would not violate that fine principle for which it stands e'en though I were reduced to the direst poverty." He paused again to give her one of his gentle smiles. "Nor, in spite of all thee says, I think, would thee."

The widow made an impatient gesture. "To be sure I wouldn't when its ideas remain within reason. 'Tis a fine thing to have a place where Christian folk who do but differ on matters of doctrine can have a chance to think as they will. But foreign Jews—folk of an entirely different race and creed—that's different."

"And how is it different?" asked Joshua. His tone was so oddly low and even it made Patrick look up into his face in quick question. It was set in a stern whiteness and his clear hazel eyes held those of the woman before him in unrelenting challenge. "I find naught in holy writ to say 'tis different. Nor do I find aught in the teaching of Him who founded the Christian faith that makes men of a different race and creed one whit less our brothers."

The widow's eyes had fallen before that clear challenging gaze, and she stood looking so chastened and distressed that, to soften the effect of his sternness, the Quaker added gently, "Nay, dear lady, much as I value your concern for me, I think there is room here for all of us."

Widow Sears shook her head, clucking her tongue as she reached in the pocket beneath her skirt for coins to pay for the candles. "You Quakers!" she said. "A body can't argue with you. No wonder you are taking the colony."

Patrick was so choked with the emotions the chandler's words had aroused in him that he could not speak. But when they were out in the street again he slipped his arm through Joshua's and they walked along thus in silence until they reached the next gate. Then, as they were about to turn into it, he found voice to stammer, "Oh, sir, it was the finest, the most generous—"

Joshua stopped him with a gesture. "What would thee expect, boy?" he asked almost with impatience. "A principle remains a principle e'en does the wind catch a man where the hair is short." Then resuming his usual genial tone he added, "Well, let us see what we will find here."

They found that there too the household had provided itself with the better candles that were just as cheap. And so it was all down the street. When all the houses in the town had been canvassed, nearly half their stock of candles remained unopened.

"Well," said the chandler with forced cheerfulness as they turned away from the last door, "we may as well be starting home now."

They left the town in silence and trudged along the wagon road the carts of Master Jenks had made between Pawtucket and the wharf in Providence from which the wares from the iron works were shipped by boat down the Bay to Newport. It was past mid-afternoon and they had left home before sunup. A cold fog had come in from the sea, creeping up the estuary and spreading out over the valley in a dank, gray cloud. Its chill seemed to strike to the very center of Patrick's being, quenching the warming fire of his admiration for the chandler's stand for his principles and the enthusiasm stirred by Roger Williams' talk. He felt as though he were sinking into a black pit of despair. Life was a heartless and terrible business, the future both immediate and as far ahead as he could fling his imagination seemed hopeless. It was well enough to have principles; but in the meantime here were these Jews, and the chandler and Hannah would lose the trade they loved. He glanced sidewise at the girl walking between himself and Joshua to see if she realized the fate that faced them.

She was trudging steadily along looking straight ahead of her, her head up and her lips pressed tight together; but slowly, steadily, one great tear after another was rolling down the cheek that was toward him and dropping off her little high-held chin.

He knew she would not want him to speak to her so he put out his hand silently and touched her arm with a gesture of sympathy. With that a great sob she was evidently suppressing by main force broke from her.

The chandler stopped suddenly and bent down to her in tender concern. "There, there, daughter," he said, drawing her to him and patting her comfortingly, "thee must not give way so. All will come out for the best in the end. Thee will see."

"I—I k-know it will, Father," sobbed the girl, "and later I shall be able to be hopeful about it too. But right now I'm so tired and so cold and so—so hungry." She ended on a pitiful wail and, leaning against her father, sobbed in good earnest.

The chandler's jaw dropped and he stared at Patrick

146

over the girl's head with a comical expression of blank consternation. "Bless my soul!" he exclaimed. "I clear forgot our mid-day meal."

Patrick burst into weakly shaken laughter of relief. So that was what was the matter with him! The black pit of despair into which he seemed sinking was only the pit of an empty stomach! "I did myself, sir," he replied, still laughing. "I was almost as near to cry as Hannah; but I did not realize 'twas hunger that ailed me."

Hannah raised her head to join in the laughter with tears still running down her cheeks.

Joshua took his kerchief from his pocket and wiped them away, scolding gently as he did so. "Why did thee not remind me, foolish child? Think how vexed thy good mother would be did she know I had let thee come to such a pass—and that after all the pains she took to pack a tasty mitchin for us. Late as it is we must stop and eat."

The suggestion seemed to restore the spirits of the two young people to normal. They were all excitement over selecting a comfortable spot by the roadside, unloading the basket from Christopher's pack, and unpacking the lunch. In a few minutes they were all eating hungrily.

As Patrick's hunger abated his hopes began to rise. After all, the chandler's present difficulty was not an uncommon one. He had come in contact with men engaged in trade in his father's house and during his work on the docks in Belfast. From their talk he judged they were always encountering difficulties they had had to overcome. Trade was good or bad according to the popularity of the wares they were able to secure, it seemed. Their constant struggle appeared to be to find out what people wanted and to get whatever it was by hook or by crook. Well, he thought,

people wanted spermaceti candles. The answer was plain—
they must find a way of getting spermaceti and making
them.

"I know what we must do, sir," he blurted out. "We
must make spermaceti candles ourselves."

The chandler broke into an amused but somewhat rueful laugh. "Now as I live," he exclaimed, "just listen to
the boy. How can we make spermaceti candles when we
have none of the stuff, have no way of getting it, and
would not know how to use it did we have a houseful?"

Patrick looked a bit taken aback for a moment; the
next an incident of his Belfast days popped into his mind
and the idea it suggested brought him bolt upright gulp-
ing with eagerness. He had become acquainted with a
youth near his own age in one of the warehouses and for
a long time had thought him a common dock-hand like
himself. But finally he had discovered he was the son of a
rival merchant and that he was working in the warehouse
of his father's competitor in the hope of discovering where
he secured his most marketable wares. "When a trade rival
has the best of you," the youth had told him with a knowing wink, "climb in his pocket."

Patrick assumed as near an imitation of that knowing
look as he could muster and, without introduction, repeated the remark verbatim.

Joshua was in the act of taking a bite of cold hasty
pudding and he paused with the morsel suspended to stare
at the boy in undisguised dismay. "What kind of talk is
this?" he demanded. "Thee sounds as though thee had
taken leave of thy senses, lad."

The boy hastened to explain, recounted the incident,
and then went on, "And I was thinking, sir, that we could

do much the same thing ourselves. I could go to Newport, take employment with these Jewish chandlers, and find out all about how they make their candles."

The chandler stared at him a moment more, then broke into a series of delighted chuckles. "Well, I declare," he brought out at length, and again, "Well, I declare!"

But the idea did not seem to please Hannah at all. "We do not want to make candles from that horrid stuff from whales," she protested. "We want to make them as we always have, from bayberry wax. There will always be folk to want the lovely, fragrant candles."

Her father shook his head. "Not enough to make a trade that would support a family, my child," he answered sadly. He sat looking into space awhile, an expression of sorrow upon his face much like the one Patrick had noted there that day on the bayberry hills as he watched Paucottauwat gazing off bitterly across the bay. "Nay," he said at length with a sigh, "we should accept with gratitude a thing that makes life easier and better for folks in general. Patrick is right in saying that are we to keep on with the chandler's trade we must make the better candles."

Patrick could not bear the look of grief on Hannah's face. "We can make both kinds," he assured her hastily, "bright ones for folk to work by and the fragrant kind to use when they want to enjoy themselves." Then he turned hopefully to Joshua again. "Say I may go, sir. I know I could contrive a way to get into the place where the candles are made."

Joshua laid his hand on the boy's knee and smiled at him with gentle question. "But look, son," he said, "there are things here an honest man must consider. The process by which the candles are made is the trade secret of these chandlers. I would feel as much a thief to filch it by stealth as to steal a man's purse outright."

The eager light in the boy's eyes flickered and died. Their gaze wandered and fell. He sat silent a moment, then said in a low, unhappy voice, "I see that now, sir, when you point it out so; but I'd not thought of it that way before."

The chandler did not answer, he seemed so deep in thoughts of his own. Presently he began to express them aloud, though more as if to himself than to the others. "Still," he said, "knowledge of these superior candles is bound to spread like wild-fire. 'Twill be no time till all will be wanting them. Then the demand will be so great one firm of chandlers cannot possibly supply it. In time they will be forced to share their secret with others." He fell silent again, thinking. "It might be," he said slowly at last, "that there would be a way by which we might be the first to whom they would pass it on."

The eagerness leapt up in Patrick's eyes again. "Aye, sir, that well might be. Please, sir, let me go and try to find the way."

Hannah was leaning forward, gazing intently at the boy as he spoke and the same strange look of far-seeing Patrick had seen in her eyes the day in the barnyard when they had talked of the bayberry wax was in them again. "He will find it," she said with quiet conviction. "I know that for certain, Father."

Joshua glanced at her questioningly, then his gaze came back to Patrick's face. "As I live," he said in a low voice, "I believe he might. Just since we have been talking here the lad has changed so. This minute he looks a man."

152

11

OFF TO NEWPORT!

NAOMI received the news of what had happened in Providence with the philosophic independence of one who has lived the self-sufficient life of a pioneer. "Let their trade go then," she told her husband with a spirited toss of her comely head. "We can get on without it. We managed here ere thee began to chandler for Providence and we can do the same again. We've a good roof above us and food sufficient so we need ne'er go hungry. Beside," she ended with a twinkle, "this leaves us such a store of candles that we'll have candlelight such as we've ne'er had in all our lives."

Joshua smiled his gratitude but shook his head in gentle disagreement. "Nay, wife," he said, " 'tis not as simple as that. A man is not content to let his trade go thus. His trade is his life. 'Tis a thing he must fight for." And then, with Patrick breaking in to make eager additions, they unfolded the plan for the boy to go to Newport.

She heard them out with the tolerant patience with which she would have listened to one of Jonathan's wild schemes. "Well, husband," she said at the end, "I know thee too well to try to dissuade thee once thy mind is set; but to my way of thinking 'tis folly for the boy to go alone. He is scarce more than a child. How can thee expect him to go to a great place like Newport and accomplish such a thing? I say that so be 'tis to be done thee should go to Newport thyself and meet these chandlers. Then does it turn out the boy is to stay, thee can see he is safely placed in a good home with Friends where we will be sure he is cared for."

The idea that he ought to go to Newport himself had already suggested itself to Joshua. " 'Tis true I'll not really rest content unless I go myself and give full assurance of our honest intent," he admitted. "But, considering what has befallen, I felt I could scarce afford the trip right now."

"But 'twould really cost thee next to naught," insisted Naomi. "Thee could stay with Friends in Newport without cost and thee would pay the Indian that took thee down the Bay with some of the wampumpeag we had on hand when the law was passed."

Patrick pricked up his ears at the odd term. "Wampumpeag," he asked, "what is that? I have read of belts of wampum, but the word 'wampumpeag' I have not seen in aught I have read."

"It means strung beads," replied Joshua. "The same kind of beads or wampum used to make the Indian's belts and ornaments also serve him as money in certain of the tribes including the Narragansetts. It is strung for convenience in counting. So wampumpeag means money. Coin was so scarce in the early settlements that the white man soon adopted it as a medium of exchange also. Eventually it became legal tender in the colonies and remained so here in Rhode Island till just some ten years since. Then a law was passed making its use between whites illegal. So now we can only use it in trade with the natives, and, as thee may have guessed from what my good wife just said, we had a goodly amount on hand when the law went into effect."

Patrick was all interest and asked eagerly if he might be permitted to see some.

"To be sure," Joshua answered, rising and going to a pine chest that stood against the wall. He took a box from it and returning to where Patrick sat, set it on the table beside him and raised the lid. It was filled to the brim with strings of beads. Some were all white, and as the boy drew one forth from the mass he estimated it must be close to two yards long. Others were made up of purple beads or varying shades of dark blue, and these were only half as long as the white strings.

Joshua took out one of the white strings also and held it up. "That is what is called a fathom. It contains three hundred and sixty beads and its value in English money used to be around sixty pence. Six beads were worth a penny. Thee will note that the dark strings are but half as long. That is because the dark wampum is made from different shell from the white and is much harder to make, so it has twice the value. The shorter dark string had the same value as the long white one."

Patrick examined the beads, admiring their wonderful symmetry and finish. In shape they were tiny cylinders about as big around as a wheat straw. They varied in length from an eighth to a half an inch and they were strung through a hole bored lengthwise through them. "But how could they ever make such things of shell?" he asked.

"The white wampum was not so difficult," replied

Joshua. " 'Tis made from the solid central shank of the periwinkle shell with the rest of the shell broken away and the shank sawed in the desired lengths. But the dark wampum is made from the shell of the quohog or hard clam, and each cylinder has to be carved out separately." He dropped the string back into the box and sat looking thoughtfully at the wampum. " 'Tis true," he said after a bit, coming back to Naomi's remark from which Patrick's question had diverted them, "I may as well use a portion of it to pay an Indian to take me to Newport and back."

"Thee was planning to go this fall in any case," Naomi reminded him.

A shadow passed across Joshua's face. He sat looking at his wife with an expression of tender sorrow a moment before he answered softly, "I was going for a special reason, thee knows that, my dear. Now that I will not have the means to bring thee back the glass I promised thee, I've no joy in the thought of the trip."

Naomi laid her hand on his with a touch of understanding. "I know, husband," she said very gently. In spite of herself she gave a little sigh. "I must admit I should dearly have loved to have the glass; but since it has fallen out that 'tis impossible I see quite plainly I did not yet deserve it." Her voice and face had the simple sweetness of a trusting child's. "So oft I was impatient when we were forced to have the shutters closed."

Suddenly Patrick saw her through a blur and he looked quickly away to hide the fact. "She shall have her glass," he said hotly within himself. "An it is the last thing I do, she shall have it."

"I scarce think thy recording angel has marked that up to thy discredit," Joshua told her in a tone of tender jesting.

She gave a little laugh which told how pleased she was by his comment and then, reverting to her briskest and most practical tone, went on, "Well, glass or no glass, I say thee should go just as thee planned a long time since."

The last words made Hannah glance quickly at her father, an eager light in her eyes. For a long time since when the trip to Newport was planned, it was decided she was to go with him to see the place for the first time. She would not ask but she waited, almost holding her breath, to see if he would remember. She did not find out because, before he could answer, her mother went on:

"Thee promised to take Hannah for the boat ride and to let her see a port and I think thee still should do so."

And so it was settled. The next day was filled with busy preparation, and the following morning before dawn the three were once more on their way to Providence.

This time when they reached the town Joshua walked on straight down its single street to the far end where a number of small boathouses were clustered along the water's edge. There were boat landings beside many of them, with a number of boats of various kinds moored beside them. Most of them were clumsy, flat-bottomed rowboats; but here or there was a trim pinnace or a sturdy, seaworthy shallop. Patrick wanted to linger to inspect them but Joshua walked quickly from one landing to another as though seeking for some special craft.

"There are some half dozen Indians who hang about here with their canoes as a rule, hoping to pick up a passenger," he explained. "But do we find none at the landings there are sure to be some at a place beyond where they beach their dugouts."

They walked on past the boathouses to a little rounded cove and there, sure enough, several canoes were drawn up in a line on the shore. There were no Indians in sight but Joshua walked on toward the boats quite undisturbed.

"There'll be someone there, of that thee can be certain. Some of them sleep in their canoes. They'd not all go off and leave their boats unguarded."

They advanced very quietly but, as they drew near, the figure of an Indian arose as though by magic from one of the dugouts. When he caught sight of them he leaped lightly ashore and stood waiting for them to come up, smiling expectantly.

Patrick noted with interest that this Indian was little older than he was himself. His head was shaved on one side but on the other the hair was long and gathered into a knot behind his ear. Patrick recalled reading this was the way Indian boys who had passed the first stage of initiation into the status of young braves were supposed to wear it. The lad was slim as a birch, his features were more delicately cut than those of Paucottauwat and reflected a keener intelligence. Altogether the impression he made was of greater grace and fineness.

"A Narragansett," thought Patrick, remembering that Joshua had described the tribe as being of an unusually high order.

Evidently the youth was pleased to see that two of his prospective passengers were so near his own age, for he cast a comradely grin at the pair of young people, then turned to Joshua and asked in English, "You want hire canoe?"

"To Newport," Joshua answered and added quickly, "How much wampum?"

The boy hesitated a split second. "Four fathom," he ventured experimentally.

The chandler smiled at him quizzically. "Down and back," he replied, as though making a statement rather than asking a question.

The Indian gave an exclamation of shocked surprise. "Down," he said positively but in a tone of sorrowful amazement that Joshua should have made such a proposal.

Joshua went on smiling, but he thrust his hand into his pocket suggestively. "Down and back," he repeated.

The youth folded his arms across his chest with a dramatic gesture and in his turn repeated, "Down!"

Hannah touched Patrick on the arm and nodded to the boat. They walked on down to the water's edge.

"We may as well get in," said the girl. "That will go on for a long time, but in the end they will come to an understanding. Indians always say more than they expect to get in the hope folk will bargain with them. They love it. He will come to Father's terms because he knows that, beyond a doubt, Father will give him more than he has asked as a gift ere they part." She paused to give an indulgent smile. "But first he must show himself too smart to be cheated by a white man."

She would have stepped into the canoe at once, but Patrick stopped to look at it with interest. "Why," he exclaimed, " 'tis made from a single log! I thought all Indians used canoes made of birch bark."

"Not most of the Algonquin tribes," the girl replied. "They all make dugouts. 'Tis a marvel to see them at work making one. The cavity is burned out with hot rocks. They heat a great lot red hot and pile them into a hole they have started in the log and leave them till the wood is charred soft and they are cold. Then they take them out and scrape away the charred substance with shell scrapers and do the same thing over again. It takes many days to get such a cavity finished."

"I should think so," answered Patrick. "And 'twas no small task to strip the log, taper the ends so gracefully, and polish the outside to such a finish. 'Tis like old ivory."

Hannah passed her hand along the side of the dugout. "Aye, it is," she agreed, "but 'tis not as lovely as the inside. The charring darkens the grain of the wood and gives it such a richness."

There was easily room in the canoe for six persons to sit in it but it had no seats. Patrick remarked upon the fact and Hannah pointed to a blanket lying in a heap within it.

"The Indian must have been wrapped in it as he slept," she suggested, "but I think 'tis meant to sit upon."

Patrick folded the blanket and laid it out neatly in the bottom of the canoe, helped Hannah in and they had just established themselves comfortably when the other two joined them, both smiling as though the argument had come out to their mutual satisfaction.

Joshua took his place with the others but the Indian shoved the canoe off from the shore first and leapt into the stern after it was afloat. A few quick strokes of his paddle sent the dugout shooting out into the estuary, Providence fell away behind them with surprising rapidity and in a moment or two more they were in mid-stream gliding swiftly southward.

The sun was well up in the heavens by that time. It was a perfect Indian summer day. The sky was an intensely clear, deep blue; the water even bluer and glinting in the

sunshine. The hills on both sides of them rolled away in endless dip and rise of richly variegated color splashed here and there with patches of the dark green of spruce or pine. And over everything hung the magic, golden haze of autumn. Patrick felt he had never seen anything so lovely.

The three young people soon fell to chatting happily among themselves. The Indian confirmed Patrick's guess that he was a Narragansett and announced his name was Wattanho. Hannah told her name, where her home was, and that her father was a candle chandler. Patrick added that he was also learning to become a chandler.

Wattanho looked puzzled. "Candle chandler," he repeated carefully. "What is that?"

Joshua smiled at him. "Why, lad, thee knows of the candle—of that I am sure because thy people have a name for it in their own language. Wequanantig, they say."

A smile of pleased recognition broke over the boy's face. "Ah," he said, nodding, "wequanantig, the lighting stick."

"And a chandler is a person who trades in a thing," Joshua went on. "A person who trades in candles is a candle chandler." He touched himself on the breast. "My trade is making candles to sell—I am a candle chandler."

"A-h-h," said Wattanho, nodding slowly as though fixing the fact in his mind. He turned to Patrick again. "You learn make candles from him?"

Patrick nodded and pointed, laughing, to Hannah. "And from her, too."

The Indian lad's dark eyes went to the girl's face with special interest. "You make candles too?" he asked.

Hannah nodded, her face breaking into one of her radiant smiles. "To be sure," she answered. "I make candles from bayberry wax."

Wattanho regarded her in smiling silence a moment, then turned to Joshua, indicating the girl with a movement of his head. "She like candle herself," he said. "She smile and make light just like candle. Indian name her 'Wequanantig Squasese.' "

Joshua's eyes rested on Hannah's smiling face with fond affection. "And a good name for her 'twould be," he agreed. "Did thee understand him, daughter? He said the Indians would name thee 'Candle Girl.' "

Hannah flushed, but her smile still lingered. Patrick looked at her and there was a strange, tight feeling in his chest.

"Candle Girl," he thought. Yes, that was just what she was.

They were out of the estuary by that time and, with Wattanho's paddle flashing with rhythmic steadiness, were slipping rapidly down the bay. Joshua pointed out the landmarks as they passed. That inlet to the east was Mount Hope Bay. The land that bordered it was Massasoit's homeland and there, at a place also called Mount Hope, Metacomet had his residence. Across the bay on the east that point was Warwick where there was another settlement. Farther to the south on the east shore were lowlands where there were great plantations similar to those in Virginia. The greatest amount of the shipping that went out of Newport came from there—cattle and sheep, wool and tobacco, and, especially, fine horses and cheeses for which the district was famous.

Presently they were skirting the eastern side of an island and Joshua told them it was named Prudence Island. Then almost at once they sighted the northern tip of Aquidneck, the island upon which Newport was located toward its southern end. For a long time they slid quietly along in the channel between the two.

The sun was nearing the western horizon when Wattanho raised his paddle and pointed ahead of them. "Newport," he announced.

Patrick looked and saw a cluster of low buildings beside a long wharf running out into the bay, and standing off from the shore another tiny rocky island. A moment later the canoe slid up beside the wharf. Wattanho brought it to a stop beside a flight of ladder-like steps which rose to the wharf and held it while they got out and went up. Then, calling up a last promise to meet Joshua there the next day for the return trip, he paddled off to the rendezvous of all the other Indian canoe-men who put into Newport.

Patrick had learned a lesson from the embarrassment his misconception of Providence had caused him, so he made no comment on his impression of Newport. But, to tell the truth, after having seen Belfast this little new port town seemed no port at all. There were several ships tied up beside the wharf, it was true, but instead of the great merchant sailing vessels of which there were always a number in port at Belfast, these were small sloops or brigantines designed for coastwise shipping or for trade between the American colonies and the Barbados. The warehouses that lined the wharf were small one or one-and-a-half story buildings instead of the great structures to which he had been accustomed.

Beyond the wharf a straggling street lined by small shops of various kinds led along the water-front. Beyond that, on a gentle rise covering a half dozen squares, lay the rest of the town.

165

Having cast a calculating eye over its dimensions, Patrick turned to Joshua and remarked with a laughing nod toward the little cluster of buildings, "Seems like we should have no trouble locating the shop of those chandlers in a town the like of that."

Joshua glanced at where the sun was about to slip into the bay. "Nay, I'd say we shouldn't, but by the time we do I fear 'twill be too late to see them today. We'd best go and seek the Friends with whom we expect to spend the night and on the morrow start to find our chandlers."

But Patrick and Hannah would not hear of the idea. "Please, Father," begged Hannah, "let's find the shop now; then on the morrow we'll know just where to go. We could ask that gentleman," she ended, pointing to a man who stood in the door of one of the warehouses.

Joshua gave in to them with laughing good humor and they all crossed to the man to make their inquiry.

"Jewish chandlers?" said the man, when they had explained what it was they were seeking. "You must mean the shop of Simon Mercedes. Mendez and Mercedes is the name it goes by; but 'tis Simon that runs it." He came out from the doorway and pointed down the wharf to the straggling street along the water-front. "That's Strand Street. The next is Shipwright. You'll know it by the shipyards. Go a square beyond them and you'll find the Mercedes shop. There's a sign on it so you can't miss it."

They thanked him and set off down the wharf. The port might be no sight to Patrick but to Hannah it was all new and wonderful. She had to stop to look at everything so their progress along the way that had been outlined for them was slow. Nevertheless it was not long until they stood before a building which bore a sign across its front that read:

MENDEZ & MERCEDES
CANDLE CHANDLERS

Compared with the small buildings about it the chandler's establishment was quite imposing—and the sign was impressive.

Joshua was really awed by it. "My, my," he exclaimed, "these chandlers must do a business."

Even Patrick was impressed.

As they stood looking at it, a boy came out to put up the shutters for the night. Joshua spoke to him and he confirmed Joshua's fear that it was too late to catch the master of the shop that day.

"We scarce expected to," Joshua assured him. "But we'll be back the first thing in the morning."

"Who shall I tell Master Mercedes to expect, sir?" asked the boy.

Joshua hesitated just a bare instant, then replied with assumed casualness, "Tell him chandlers from Providence —that will be sufficient."

"No names, sir?" said the boy. His brows were raised and there was a note in his voice which subtly conveyed the impression that to leave no names would mark them as persons of no consequence whatever.

"The names are no matter," Joshua answered evasively. "Master Mercedes would not know them in any case."

Patrick noted both the hesitation and the evasion—and knew exactly what they meant. For the first time the fact of his namelessness struck home to him. He was a nobody!

He didn't even have a name he could give to a common hireling. The fact made him feel mean beyond expression and lost and desolate. When they turned back into the street, he walked along with his eyes on the ground, ashamed even to look at Hannah or the chandler.

Presently he felt an arm laid gently about his shoulders. He glanced up and found Joshua looking down at him, a pucker of trouble between his brows.

"What are we to do about this, Patrick lad?" he asked gently. Then without waiting for the boy to reply he went on, "I've not troubled myself about thy having no name ere this, for at home it made no difference. But thee sees how it is now that thee is to be out in the world. Thee must have a name, boy." He paused as though expecting Patrick to make some response, and when he did not he resumed with a sigh, "Little as thee likes it, lad, I think thee will have to resurrect thy name from the sea."

Patrick did not reply but walked along thinking of the matter. After all, he thought, why not? Few here in America would know the name anyhow. He said it over in his mind—his father's name, a name familiar to thousands in the British Isles—a name before which hundreds had trembled and for which hundreds more had nothing but hatred. And his own mind recoiled from it with a hatred that seemed a heaped-up total of all those bitter fears and hates.

He looked up at Joshua, shaking his head. "Nay, sir," he said in a bleak voice, "I cannot do it. That name is too much connected with the things I hate. Better far to be nameless."

Joshua patted the shoulder under his hand and they walked on in silence for a while. "I understand thy feeling, lad," Joshua said finally, "but truly thee must have a name." He hesitated a moment and then went on, "And since thee will not use thy own, what would thee think of taking mine?"

The boy did not answer—not because he did not wish to but because he was choked by the relief and gratitude that welled up within him.

"Mapes is not an aristocratic name," the chandler continued, "such as I venture was thy own; but 'tis of good lineage—and, as far as I know, there is no blot upon it."

Patrick found his voice quickly at that. "Oh, sir," he cried, "all I need to know is that it is your name. I'll be proud to bear it, and I'll try to put no blot upon it, sir."

Joshua gave his shoulders a little squeeze. "Thee won't, lad. Of that I'm certain." He broke into a gentle chuckle. "In fact, I've a notion thee will bring the name up in the world quite notably."

Patrick smiled up at him. They exchanged a look of man-to-man understanding. Then they walked on again in silence. But Patrick's head was up now.

The lost and desolate feeling was gone. He was somebody. He was somebody with a name that had no blot of cruel intolerance upon it. He said the name over to himself experimentally. "Patrick Mapes." Yes, it was a good name. It sounded substantial and rather important.

His mind ran forward into the future, picturing what his life under that name might be like. Presently he gave a pleased little laugh.

"What is it, lad?" asked Joshua.

"I was thinking what a good thing 'twill be for our business when I am your partner that I have the name of Mapes," he replied. "One day we'll have a fine shop like

Master Mercedes and our names will make an even better sign than his." He stopped and stood looking off at nothing with narrowed eyes as though actually seeing it. He gave another gratified little laugh. "I can see it now just as plain with my mind's eye—all printed out in great, brave letters." His voice took on an impressively dramatic tone as though reading what he saw:

"MAPES & MAPES
CANDLE CHANDLERS."

12

CANDLES TWICE AS BRIGHT

THE shutters of Simon Mercedes' shop had hardly been taken down the next morning when Joshua and his two young companions arrived. A few minutes later they were sitting in a little office at the front of the shop and Joshua was telling its master the story of the events which had caused them to come to see him.

Patrick had been prepared to dislike the man who had brought such difficulty on Joshua and his family. He had pictured him as a heartless and grasping creature trampling ruthlessly on other men in his climb to business success. Now as he sat watching him listening to Joshua's story, he could not but see that this man was anything but heartless. He was a little man with a manner almost timid in its gentleness. There was great kindness in his soft brown eyes and the fineness of his dark features betrayed a nature too sensitive for comfort. As Joshua's tale progressed, a pained and helpless distress was written more and more plainly upon his face. At its close he looked from one to the other of the little group with such hurt and poignant pleading in his eyes that Patrick's heart melted with pity for him. His look gave the boy the feeling that he had seen so much suffering he could not endure to witness another grief or sorrow.

"Please, my friends," he said in quaint broken English, "you must believe me. I have not meant to hurt any man's trade. We Jews have suffered so much we would not want to hurt anyone. And surely not one here in this colony. We were not welcome anywhere till we were given sanctuary here."

Joshua's face was flooded with sympathetic understanding. "We are brothers in that regard, my friend," he said gently. "I, too, am a refugee from persecution. My young wife and I were in like case with thyself when we arrived in America." He went on to tell his own experience briefly.

Tears stood in the other man's eyes when he finished. He wiped them away openly and without shame. "Ah, then you can understand how we Jews feel for this colony. We are so grateful we wish to do all we can to make it prosper. The secret of making spermaceti candles is known to us in our own country. We feel that better light to work by and to read good books is needed here so we decided to introduce them." He paused to look pleadingly about. "But I do not wish to spoil the trade of other chandlers. I would rather give up making the candles."

The Quaker made a gesture of quick protest. "Oh, sir, believe me, we had no such thought. A thing that serves life as does better light must be given every help to grow. But what we felt was this: the demand for the candles will soon outstrip the facility of thy firm to provide them. Then the secret of how they are made will have to be passed on to other chandlers. We hoped we might be among the first to share it and, looking forward to that day, my boy here felt he would like to be learning something of thy methods. In short, sir, he would like a place with thee."

Simon Mercedes shot a quick, penetrating look at Patrick. And the boy felt that in that one look he had taken stock of him completely. For the first time he saw that behind the gentleness of the man there was a mind of a rapier-like keenness.

"Well," he said guardedly, " 'tis not impossible I could use a boy. Tell me about yourself, lad—I mean what education you have had, what training and experience."

Patrick did so, feeling almost as if it were unnecessary.

"So," he exclaimed when the boy mentioned his experience in Belfast, "you have seen the world also! That would be helpful. Our work is quite different from what you have been doing with Master Mapes, but you could learn, no doubt." He seemed to reflect a moment, then sat forward, his hands on his knees as though about to rise. "Suppose I show you all about our shop, then we can decide." He glanced at Joshua. "You would like that, eh?"

Joshua had hardly expected such a thing in view of the fact the method was supposed to be a secret. "To be sure," he replied with some surprise, "so be 'tis agreeable to thee."

The other man rose, smiling. "Why not, why not?" he answered with a shrug. " 'Twould take much more than looking for a man to learn how to treat spermaceti. This way," he added and opened the door into a great room beyond.

Patrick had pictured a shop which would look something like Joshua's home workroom when candle making was in full swing only much larger and more elaborate. But there was nothing about the room to suggest that the work going on in it was even remotely connected with candle making. Tiers of casks lined the wall at the back.

On one side stood a row of heavy wooden implements he thought did not look unlike the cheese presses he had seen in his father's dairy room. On the other, the wall was lined with low brick furnaces upon which a dozen great iron caldrons were steaming. The air was thick with the smell of hot oil and sharp with some other acrid odor.

Joshua stood staring about with an expression rather like a lost child's. Hannah clung to his arm, amazement and disapproval written in every line of her face, her fine little nose wrinkled in distaste for the unpleasant smell.

The master of the shop waved his hand toward the implements Patrick had thought looked like cheese presses. "'Tis here the spermaceti in the whale oil is extracted as it comes from the try works," he told them.

"From the whale oil," echoed Joshua questioningly. "'Twas my impression the stuff was a semi-solid only found by itself in the head."

"So most think," replied Simon Mercedes. "For years e'en expert whalers thought so. But eventually we learned it was present in a slightly different form all through the great blanket of blubber with which the whale's body is covered. Till that was discovered the making of spermaceti candles was not practical, since the amount obtained from one whale was so small their price would have had to be too great. Now, after the oil is tried out, the spermaceti can be extracted from it without injuring any of its uses in the least and the amount is large enough so that when it is added to the head matter the total is sufficient to make it possible to produce candles which can sell at a moderate price."

"I was wondering how 'twas possible they could be made to sell at a price no greater than tallow candles," said Patrick. "I see now 'tis because the spermaceti you get from the oil is only a—a—" He faltered, trying to recall an expression he had heard merchants use. It came at last. "A by-product," he ended triumphantly.

Once more Master Mercedes gave him a penetrating glance. But this time there was a pleased light in his eye. "Exactly," he replied. Then he turned to Joshua and, cocking his head toward the boy, added, "A smart lad that."

A smile of fatherly pride broke over Joshua's face. "I think so," he said quietly.

Patrick felt something warm creeping up all over him from his toes to the very roots of his hair. To hide his emotion he pointed to the furnaces with their steaming caldrons and inquired as casually as he could what their use might be.

" 'Tis there the spermaceti is refined and bleached. For in its crude state 'tis far from the pure white stuff you see in the finished candle." He crossed to a vat and returned with a lump of something that looked rather like very dirty bread dough with some sparkling substance sprinkled through it. "That's as it looks ere 'tis bleached." He turned to Hannah with a smile of suppressed amusement. "It takes a bad smell sometimes to get a thing purified."

A flood of pink swept up to the edge of the girl's hood. She had not been aware their host was noting her distaste for the smell of his product and, taken thus by surprise, she could think of nothing to say and only stood blushing miserably.

Patrick came quickly to her assistance. "Hannah thinks

all candles should smell like bayberry," he said, laughing.

To his surprise his jesting remark brought an expression of pensive thoughtfulness into Simon Mercedes' eyes. "And she is right," he said. "No doubt they should. But—" he gave a resigned shrug—"life is a compromise. We yield up one thing to gain another. We must sacrifice fragrance, it seems, to have the better light."

That reminded Hannah of something she really had wanted to ask. "Might—might we see one of the candles lighted, sir?" she hesitated. "I have heard folk talk of the marvel of their brightness and I would dearly love to see it for myself."

"To be sure you may," he answered, smiling. "But first you must see the candles. This is the molding room," he told them, opening another door. Then, as he ushered them in, he added to Joshua as though all the time he had noted his lost child look, "You will feel more at home here, sir."

Joshua looked about him and gave a rueful laugh. "Well, not much more at home, I'm bound to admit."

A half dozen workers were busy pouring the liquid spermaceti into molds that made Joshua's molds, of which he was so proud because they would turn out two dozen candles at a time, look like toys. There were gigantic caldrons set on brick furnaces to keep it melted, and when the candles in one of the molds were hardened they were lifted out dozens at a time in long rows raised from the molds by levers.

At first the magnitude of everything gave Joshua a dazed feeling; but as he watched his imagination took fire. It would be wonderful, he thought, to be the master of such a shop—to feel oneself responsible for such hundreds of candles coming into being as if by magic. He drew a long tremulous breath. "Thee must be a proud man, Master Mercedes," he said in a hushed voice.

The look of distress that had been in Simon Mercedes' face as he sat in his little office and listened to Joshua tell why they were there returned to it. He shook his head. "Nay, my friend, I am not proud—not when men such as you have cause to complain of me. I'll take no joy in what I'm doing here till that wrong is righted. But you can understand there is much to be discussed with my partner and many things to be settled first. In the meantime the boy can stay. He is a sharp lad with eyes in his head. What he sees for himself here—" He let an eloquent shrug finish the sentence more significantly than words.

Joshua began a faltering expression of his thanks, but he stopped him with a gesture. " 'Tis only justice, my friend, and for any man I would feel forced to make some arrangement. For you, Master Mapes, I do it out of a full heart. You, like myself, have found refuge here after knowing what it is to be hounded from place to place and to see no welcoming beacon in the gloom. Not for anything would I have that refuge made desolate. We will find a way to save your trade—trust me for that."

He held out his hand and Joshua took it silently. They stood looking into each other's eyes exchanging the wordless pledge of men who have come through trial to a deeper understanding of man's responsibility to his fellows.

When the handclasp ended, Simon Mercedes turned smiling to Hannah. "And now, young lady," he said, "we light the candle." He stepped to one of the benches, took one from a pile lying there, went to the furnace, and lighted it. "You cannot judge of the light here in the day-light," he told them. "There is a store closet that is dark. I will take you in there."

He ushered them into a windowless room, closed the door behind them, and stood holding the candle aloft. Everything in the room was visible almost as though in daylight. There were no dusky corners as there would have been by the light of an ordinary candle. The walls were lined with shelves piled with boxes and Hannah found she could even read the labels upon them.

" 'Tis true," she said in an awed voice, "the light *is* twice as bright." Then suddenly her eyes flew wide with some inspiring thought. She turned to Joshua. "Oh, Father," she cried, "we must make candles of the sort. Think how sovereign they'd be to use as traveler's candles."

Simon Mercedes' brows went up in smiling question. "Traveler's candles," he repeated, "and what sort of candles are those?"

Hannah explained and then went on to tell how for more years than she was old such a candle had been set each night in the window of her father's house as a beacon of hospitality to wayfarers on their lonely trail.

"Were it not for that fact," Patrick added, "I'd not be here today." He told the story of how he had taken refuge in the chandler's house. "And as you see," he ended, "that candle proved, for me, a beacon to a new life."

" 'A beacon to a new life,' " Simon Mercedes repeated in a musing voice. His eyes were dark with thought in the light of the candle. They turned to Joshua, a meaningful little smile lighting his face. "So he, too, is one of us. Here we are three who have found a new life in this place—and we are but few of many." A light of prophecy came into his eyes. "And there are thousands yet to come. This place will be like your candle, my friend—a traveler's candle to a whole world dark with intolerance, a beacon of hope to those that travel through its night."

13

OMINOUS WINTER

THE little house where Hannah had spent her entire life in complete content seemed strangely desolate to the girl when she came back to it without Patrick. They had left the boy in a good home with a Quaker family and entering upon his work in the shop of Simon Mercedes with an enthusiasm Hannah had now come to share. She was quite in accord with the plan that had taken him from them, but his vacant place in the household seemed to leave an aching gap oddly out of proportion to the length of time he had filled it.

"It scarce seems possible we should miss him so when he was here so short a time," she said to her father the next day after their return.

Joshua smiled at her with a sort of special tenderness Hannah had never noted in his look before. "The heart has its own way of counting time, my child," he answered, and there was something in his tone that made a flush rise to the girl's cheeks though she hardly knew why.

On the trip back, Joshua had made arrangements with Wattanho to go to see Patrick whenever he put into Newport with a passenger in order that the boy might send a letter back to Providence by him. His instructions had been that the Indian youth was to leave the letter at the house of Roger Williams, and Joshua had intended to go into Providence at the end of the month to get it. But long before that time Wattanho appeared upon the Mapes doorstep.

"I like come," he assured them, smiling broadly when Joshua explained he had not expected him to bring the letter all the way to their hilltop from Providence. "I come all times I got letter."

Joshua understood Indians well enough to know that the lad's willingness to make the journey to them came partly from friendliness and partly from an interest in the wampumpeag with which his Quaker passenger had been so generous at their last meeting. His coming would make it possible to get letters from Patrick at more frequent intervals and, since there was an abundant supply of wampumpeag with which to reward him, it was so arranged. Whether he actually did have passengers for Newport as often as he went there to bring back a letter thereafter, they doubted but did not care to ask. It was too good to be hearing regularly from Patrick.

The first letter told of the kind of work he was doing, of Simon Mercedes' kindness and generosity, and ended reassuringly: "I cannot but feel he intends I shall come to know all the secrets of handling spermaceti, for he hides naught from me and, in fact, seems to do all he can to put me in the way of learning everything."

Later letters gave definite information in regard to things he had found out. "The odd wooden implements I thought resembled cheese presses are really used in much the same manner," he wrote. "When the oil is semi-solid from cold, it is shoveled into sacks and these are placed in the presses and the oil pressed out just as whey is pressed from the cheese curd, leaving the spermaceti in the sacks just as the curd is left. I have seen it done once but they tell me it has to be repeated at intervals all through the winter and that the spermaceti is not entirely freed from the oil till a final spring pressing."

In another he explained the use of the great caldrons the odor of which had so offended Hannah. "The part of the vile smell not due to the hot oil itself is alkali used for bleaching. After it has served its purpose, it must be driven off as steam by long boiling. The steam from those caldrons we saw was mostly alkali. No wonder they have a vile smell."

By the end of the second month the letters began to be full of plans for the future. "We would not be ready for some time to produce spermaceti ourselves," he wrote, "but can I find a way of securing a sufficient amount of the finished product by next fall, I see no reason we could not turn out all the spermaceti candles Providence would use."

Hannah gave an involuntary little cry of gladness when her father read that phrase aloud. "That would mean he plans to come home for good by next fall, wouldn't it, Father?" she asked eagerly.

In his own mind Joshua did not see how the thing was to be possible, but he could not bear to dash the girl's hopes so he answered guardedly, "I'd judge that to be his meaning, daughter."

The girl had been spinning wick faithfully every day, but the uncertainty of their situation had made it hard for her to put any real heart into the work. That letter made spinning wick an entirely different matter. If they

were to supply all the spermaceti candles Providence would use, they would need all the wick they could possibly produce. After that the purr of the flax wheel filled the room early and late. Its gentle sound seemed a quiet little song of hope and happy expectation.

Long before that time Joshua had put oiled paper over the window openings. On the mildest days and during the warmest midday hours they could have the shutters open and a faint yellow light came in. But when it was cold, the shutters had to be closed and there was only the dim light from the one glassed window. But no matter how dim the light, Naomi never fretted now. It would have been easier for Joshua if she had. The sight of her bending patiently over her work, straining to see, or lighting a candle without comment when it was still daylight outside, was a constant poignant reminder of the misfortune which had made the provision of glass for their windows impossible.

In other ways it had little effect upon their lives. There was corn enough for meal for the winter, an abundant supply of dried beans, a store of turnips and pumpkins in the cellar; crocks of various sauces made from wild grapes, plums, and berries on the shelves; strings of dried apple and pumpkin hung from the rafters and quantities of nuts Jonathan had gathered in the fall laid out on boards placed across them. The cow in the barn provided all the milk they could use. There was fish in the river and game of many kinds in the woods. No, as Naomi had insisted, there was little danger they would go hungry.

And winter was kind to them that year. No heavy snow came till after mid-December. Frequent travelers passed along their trail and stopped to stay the night, sometimes remaining to eat the morning meal with them and give them news of the outside world.

Wattanho came regularly with letters from Patrick, but after mid-November each time as he was leaving he warned them this visit might be the last for the winter. For when bitter weather set in, he said, canoe travel to Newport would no longer be possible.

Hannah had never minded the months they were snowed in upon their hilltop. There was something cozy and snug in the sense of protected isolation. But this year she watched the sky, almost praying for it to hold back its burden of snow as long as could be. For a week more the clear weather held. Then, one morning, they woke to find their hilltop blanketed with white and every trace of the trail wiped out. Hannah gazed out disconsolately at that trackless expanse. There had been no letter from Patrick since early in the month and they had been expecting Wattanho daily.

"He'll not come now, I venture," she thought unhappily.

But she was wrong. Before the morning was over he arrived on snowshoes. And he not only had the hoped-for letter but a large package strapped pack-wise to his back.

"Patreek send," he announced, loosing the carrying thongs and lowering the package carefully to the floor.

"Now, I declare," exclaimed Naomi, "whatever could that be?"

Hannah and Joshua exchanged glances as though they already had a suspicion.

" 'Twill take but a moment to find out," laughed Joshua, starting to remove the wrappings.

As the last covering came off, Naomi gave one cry of

pure joy and then stood with clasped hands looking as though she were seeing the gates of Heaven open. The package contained two squares of leaded glass all neatly framed and ready to fit into the window holes. She had been patient with the dim light since fall and now here was her reward.

That was Wattanho's last visit. He bade them farewell before he left as though he never expected to see them again. Hannah reminded him laughing that of course he would be back in the spring, but he only gave her an odd, sober smile and made no answer.

They stood in the doorway and watched him disappear over the western hilltop, a tiny spot of black in a vast white world. He was their last visitor for more than two months of silent isolation.

Mid-March brought thawing weather, the return of travelers upon the trail, and with them disturbing news from Plymouth. A traveler who came from there remained especially to tell them what had happened so they could be prepared for any trouble that might arise because of it.

In early December, he said, a Christianized Indian named John Sausamon, who had been educated in English at the school for Indians at Natick and who, because of his ability to read and write English, had been employed as secretary and interpreter by King Philip, had come to the Assistants of the Colony with an alarming tale which he told them under pledge that they would keep his coming secret.

"For he said," the man went on, "that did Philip e'er come to know he'd come to the English with such a tale he would of a certainty be killed. He'd had a sovereign chance to learn of the sachem's intents and was mortal certain Philip was trying to draw all the tribes hereabout into a plot for a general uprising in which he hoped to wipe out the English."

Joshua did not look deeply impressed. " 'Tis the same old story," he said in a weary tone when the man had finished. "Like suspicion has been visited upon Metacomet a dozen times. Beyond doubt he was once more summoned to appear before the General Court for questioning."

The visitor gave a short, significant laugh. "He didn't have to be summoned. He came posthaste of his own accord. Somehow he must have got wind of the fact that Sausamon had told more than he should. He protested his faithfulness and pled with tears that his dear friends wouldn't believe bad stories about him." He paused to spread his hands with a meaningful shrug. "The Assistants had no proof of Sausamon's story. It was the word of one Indian against another, so they let Philip go all friendly as you please with but a warning to keep the peace. They hoped that so be there was any truth in the tale of the plot, knowing they were warned of it would cause Philip to give over his plans and that would be the end o' the matter."

"But it was not, I take it," said Joshua.

"Not by far," answered the other man. "Within a fortnight Sausamon turned up missing and, search being made for him, his body was found under the ice of a pond. The Indians tried to make it seem he had fallen in while fishing and been drowned. But another Indian came in to confess to having seen Sausamon killed there by three Wampanoags known to be right-hand men of Philip. Plainly the very thing he feared had happened to him. But," he ended with a gratified nod, "the murderers have been caught and are now jailed in Plymouth awaiting trial."

Once again Joshua gave a weary sigh. "My friend," he asked, "does thee, perchance, recall the events that led to the Pequot War? They were not dissimilar. Had the colonists been content then to leave the Indian's law to take its course, that bitter conflict might have been averted. From the Indian's point of view this Sausamon was duly executed by order of his sovereign for an act of high treason to his own people. Were I one of the Assistants," he ended, looking challengingly at his visitor, "I confess I should counsel taking the stand that the affair was altogether an Indian matter and have naught more to do with it."

The other man stared at him with an expression of shocked horror. "Man alive," he exclaimed, "did the English take such a stand they'd ne'er be able to keep the whip hand of the natives."

Joshua looked back at him no whit disconcerted by his horror. "A whip hand cannot keep the Indians at peace," he answered in a level voice. "The hand of trust and friendship, given with the respect due a people into whose homeland we have intruded, served well in that regard in the early days at Plymouth—and," he ended pointedly, "I think 'twould still do so."

The visitor's only answer was a snort of disgusted dissent, and shortly after he took his departure.

When he was gone, Hannah came to her father and looked up into his face with anxious eyes. "Tell me truly, Father," she begged, "does thee put any credence in this story of a plot?"

He did not answer at once and when he did his voice

was thoughtfully grave. "Aye, in a way I fear I do, daughter," he replied. "A ruling monarch of any land would be more than human did he not, at times, feel an overpowering desire to rise up and wipe out interlopers with a notion they should have a whip hand. Metacomet beyond doubt has such a feeling. But to attempt it would be madness. Our hope of safety is that he may know that. However, I have no alarm for the present," he ended more cheerfully, "for I feel sure were any such thing threatening immediately that Paucottauwat would come and tell me."

The trial of the Indians accused of Sausamon's murder could not take place till the spring sitting of the General Court at Plymouth. The feeling that the future attitude of the Pokanokets depended on its outcome hung heavy in the air. The weeks dragged by in tense waiting with the red men and the white watching each other in wary hostility.

The sense of strain rested like a dead weight on Hannah. She felt it the more keenly because they were also waiting for a letter from Patrick. Wattanho had not resumed his visits with the return of open weather as they had expected, and nearly a month had gone by since canoe travel down the bay had become possible. Each morning she woke thinking, "Surely Wattanho will come today," and all day long every sound outside the door brought her to it in eager expectancy.

Then one evening just as they were getting ready to set the traveler's candle and go to bed, not Wattanho, but Patrick himself appeared. After the surprised and joyous greetings were over, questions as to how he came to be there and why he had sent no letter flew thick and fast.

"I came because I could find no way of sending a letter," the boy replied when he could get a chance to speak. "Wattanho is no longer plying his canoe on the bay. He has gone to the fortified village of the Narragansetts somewhere southward of Pettaquamscott for training with the young men of the tribe who are to become braves in the fall."

"Oh," Hannah exclaimed, "that explains why he bade us good-by as he did the last time he was here and brought the glass," and she went on to tell of Wattanho's odd smile when she had suggested he would be back in the spring.

Patrick had no chance to answer at once for reference to the glass reminded them all to express their thanks for the gift and to tell how much comfort it had given them during the dreary weeks that had passed since its coming.

Hannah bore her share in the happy talk about the gift, but she was watching Patrick with troubled, questioning eyes as she did so. For she had seen a look of arrested attention and special interest come into his face when she spoke of Wattanho's farewell, and afterward beneath the happiness of seeing them all again and the pleasure at their joy in his gift, she was sure she detected a hidden anxiety.

As soon as she could, she brought the conversation back to what he had told regarding the change in the life of the Indian youth, asking when Wattanho had gone and if he had seemed happy to do so. When Patrick had answered those questions, she added curiously, "But why shouldn't he have told us he was going away instead of just looking so strange?"

"Why does an Indian do anything?" the boy replied with a shrug. "I've not yet found out. But perchance 'twas because he feared, should he talk at all, he might let out

191

other things he'd no business to."

Joshua caught up the last words quickly. "Other things he'd no business to," he repeated questioningly. "What does thee mean, lad?"

Patrick hesitated before answering as though trying to make up his mind what he ought to say and finally, instead of giving a reply at all, asked another question. "Has there been any rumor here of late, sir, of trouble brewing with the Indians?"

Joshua looked at him sharply. "Aye, there has been, lad. Why does thee ask?"

"Because I've heard something of it in Newport and I wondered how much you knew of the matter."

"Enough not to like it," answered Joshua. And he went on to give a terse account of the events John Sausamon had set into motion and of the pending trial of the Indians accused of his killing. "Does the Court convict the fellows, I'm fearful we'll have trouble whether there was truth in Sausamon's tale of a conspiracy or not."

The anxiety the boy had been hiding was written plainly on his face now. "I believe there is truth in it, sir," he said in a tense voice. "Wattanho said things without meaning to that make me think so. He told me there were a lot of Wampanoag women and children among his people now. Wouldn't that look as though the tribesmen close enough to Metacomet to know his plans had sent their wives and children out of their territory because they knew there would soon be war there?"

Joshua looked thoughtfully anxious also. "It might," he admitted.

"Another time," Patrick resumed, "he told me that a lot of the young men of his age were in great haste to become warriors, for they thought there would soon be a chance for them to go on the warpath and win much glory."

"But surely the Narragansetts wouldn't join in a war," Hannah broke in. "They have had naught but just and friendly treatment here in this colony."

"The folk in Newport are saying that the tribe will hold to its peace treaty but that a lot of their young warriors will go with the Pokanokets just to be fighting. Everyone seems to feel a war is bound to come ere long." He paused and looked seriously about the circle of faces. "That is really the reason I came just now. I wanted to beg you all to come back to Newport with me. So be there should be fighting in Rhode Island at all, 'twould be in this end of the colony. In Newport you would be safe."

Hannah's face reflected a mixture of feelings. Patrick's proposal that they should all come to Newport with him had sent her heart leaping into her throat with joy and excitement. But before he was done speaking, it had come over her with complete certainty that, of course, they could not go. "But, Patrick," she said in an unhappy voice, "thee knows quite well we cannot leave here. We must stay to set the traveler's candle."

Patrick had thought of the traveler's candle himself. It made him sad beyond saying to think of the little house from which it had always shed its beams standing dark and deserted sending no welcoming light out upon the trail. "I know," he admitted, " 'tis hard to think of the candle not being here. But better that than that you should all be in danger."

His concern for them had touched Naomi's warm heart to its very core. Tears stood in her eyes and when she spoke her voice was husky with feeling. "There's little chance we'd be in danger, son," she told him gently and all she felt for him was in that final word. " 'Twould be folly to go off and leave our house and garden and orchard to go to ruin just because of talk that may well come to naught."

The boy looked pleadingly at Joshua seeking support, but the chandler shook his head with a little rueful laugh.

"Why, lad, I'd feel the meanest poltroon, slinking off like a frightened mouse at the first hint of uncertain danger. But thee may put thy mind at rest about us for the present, of that I am sure," and he went on once more to voice his conviction that if danger were impending, Paucottauwat would have warned him.

"But he didn't really promise to, sir," Patrick reminded him. "Don't you recall? You tried to make him and he just sat there a long time saying naught and when he did speak at length he only said something about not forgetting you."

"I recall," Joshua answered, and there was just a hint of impatience in his voice. "That was but his own way of giving his pledge. Indians do not say aye and nay as we do."

Patrick was not convinced, but the hint of impatience in Joshua's tone warned him it was useless to argue farther. "Perchance," he said, and let the matter drop for the time.

But not altogether. He remained with them three days, and each day he renewed his plea that they should come away with him. By the third evening he was convinced his mission was hopeless. So the next morning before sunup he stood on the doorstep ready to start alone on the journey back to Newport.

All the family had come out with him to see him on his

194

way. The last farewell was said. He turned reluctantly away and started off along the trail. But it was all he could do to keep his feet moving forward. Suppose he should never see them again, he thought. What if this was the last time! The thought made him turn round for one last glimpse of them. They had all gone back into the house but Hannah. She stood there alone upon the doorstep looking after him with her heart in her eyes. But when he turned, as though she knew how great his need was of cheer and encouragement, she waved to him almost gaily and sent him one of those radiant, beaming smiles which seemed so much a giving of the light within herself.

The sight of her standing there sending forth that light to him brought a lump into Patrick's throat. He recalled the name Wattanho had given her. "Wequanantig Squasese," he said softly to himself as he waved back, trying to look as brave as she.

"Good-by, Candle Girl," he called, forcing his voice to have a playful sound. Then he turned away and started on again repeating the name as he went.

Deep down within himself somewhere—too deep even for thought—he felt dimly that to him she would always be a light, a light to cheer and guide him all his life long.

14

THE MESSAGE OF HIRAM'S MILL

SPRING brought little of its usual joy to a large part of New England that year. Rumors betraying the apprehension hanging over the countryside for miles around reached the Mapes hilltop with disturbing regularity. Many of them were fantastic tales which Joshua brushed aside with a laugh. But after the trial at which the Wampanoags accused of killing John Sausamon were found guilty of murder and condemned to death, some of the stories seemed really to warrant alarm. One traveler whose home was on the Mount Hope peninsula not far from King Philip's village told of being wakened in the night by the rhythmic thud of drums and the strange, wild whoops which accompanied the Indians' war dance. Another told of having seen passing bands of strange warriors belonging to tribes not native to the district.

That last report made Joshua look more grave than any of the others. "An that is true," he said, "it gives substance to the rumor of a conspiracy."

Events after the eighth of June, when the convicted men were executed according to the English law, seemed to bear out his fear. For immediately small bands of maddened Indians, made up not only of Wampanoags but of Nipmucks, Saconets, and Pocassetts as well, swarmed over the country venting their wrath in attacks not upon the English population but upon their property. Barns were burned, houses were rifled in the absence of their owners, corn and other provisions were stolen.

It was Master Jenks who brought news of many of these occurrences. He had come to inform them that the people of the neighborhood had finally voted to convert his mill into a defensible house and to ask Joshua to volunteer his help with the work of cutting and preparing the timber required to cover the outside walls with a double thickness of great squared logs. He was boiling over with wrath at the depredations.

"Do any of the varmints come round my place doin' the like, I'll show 'em," he blustered. "Why someone hasn't filled some of 'em with lead ere this is more than I can see."

"Had they done so," Joshua replied, "they would have been doing just what those of the tribesmen most earnest for war desire. Years past at one of the times when Metacomet was summoned to Plymouth he made an oath that the Pokanokets would not be first to spill blood in war with the whites. These nuisance raids are plainly being made with the hope of provoking some outraged white into shedding Indian blood. Then they could take the warpath without violating the oath of their sachem. It behooves us all now to keep a curb on our tempers. In spite of the fact that other tribes seem to have thrown in their lot with the Wampanoags now, I've reason to believe that e'en though Metacomet may have hankered for an uprising he'd no intent or plans to start one this long time yet."

Hannah knew the reason to which he referred was his

cherished belief that Paucottauwat would have warned him of an actual plot of conspiracy. But Master Jenks did not ask him to state it, his interest centering instead on Joshua's idea of what had caused the immediate crisis.

"You mean this Sausamon matter has brought things to a head sooner than he planned?" he inquired.

"Much sooner," replied Joshua. "The hottest of his fighting men have got out of hand now, but do we let them work off their fury unharmed, this gust may blow by and we may be able to make peaceable terms with Metacomet."

Master Jenks replied to that only with an eloquent gesture and a disgusted "Faugh!" Then he reverted once more to the matter of the defensible house.

Joshua promised his aid but after a moment's hesitation added, "I'll help because I see it the neighborly thing to do, but did I not voice my own stand in the matter I'd feel myself false to my faith. And the truth is that for myself and my family I put no trust in the protection of such a fortress. I put it rather in the trust and friendliness that has e'er existed between myself and my red neighbors. Understand me," he added quickly as he saw the other man was about to make some indignant answer, "I do not expect others to feel as I do, so I will come on the morrow to help with the work and bring my boy and my horse as well."

After that Joshua and Jonathan started off for Pawtucket early each morning, and Hannah and Naomi were alone on their hilltop all the long day. Hannah told herself firmly there was really nothing to fear, yet sometimes in the stillness of a golden June morning she would find herself laying aside her work to go to the door and gaze off across the sunny clearing into the shadows of the woods on the farther hills as though she expected to find some danger lurking there. Actually she did not. But hundreds of women for miles about were peering out thus into the shadows beyond their clearings, and she could not quite rise above the infection of the general fear.

Each night Joshua brought home the news told by the neighbors who were working on the mill. None of it was good until after the middle of the month. Then one evening he came in bearing the heartening tidings that the Rhode Island government had offered its good offices as peacemaker and that Philip had consented to meet with its representatives for a parley.

" 'Tis hoped they'll be able to persuade him to let them arbitrate his differences with the English," he went on, "and since of the five from our Plantation who are to meet with him the largest number will be Friends whose repute with the natives is for friendliness and fair dealing, I think there's a fair chance they'll succeed."

Hannah's eyes glowed with happy relief. "Why, that's the very thing thee had in mind to do when thee urged Paucottauwat to come to thee with word of it should he learn Metacomet was planning war, wasn't it, Father?" she asked eagerly.

"Aye, it was, daughter," Joshua replied. "And since he hasn't come I still have hopes that things are not at as bad a pass as folk think."

But when he came home the second evening after the meeting had taken place, the distress and sorrow written on his face told them without words that report of it had reached Pawtucket and that the news was of failure.

"Metacomet and his council would commit themselves

to no engagement," he told them when they pressed him for details. He sat in silence a little, looking as though he were forcing himself to the acceptance of some bitter truth. At length he passed his hand across his eyes and said with a sigh, "I understand now why Paucottauwat has not come to me. He knew it would be useless. And I know too now that Patrick was right. He ne'er did promise to come. He couldn't. He knew what was to come and he was committed to his own people."

Within the next few days the Pokanokets gave an answer to the English more definite than any words. Up to that time only barns had been burned. On the next day after the unsuccessful parley they started burning houses. Reports of homes in ruins came from several different villages. And in one instance the news was far more disturbing than simply the tale of a home destroyed. The outraged householder had fired at the marauders and one young brave had been killed.

Joshua told the story to the anxiously listening family. "We may expect anything now," he ended. "Indian blood has been spilled by a white man. Metacomet is released from his oath. The Pokanokets are free to do as they will."

All through the years it had been the custom of the Puritan settlements to meet every crisis by proclaiming a day of fasting and prayer. All other help having failed they decided to turn to the Most High. So both Massachusetts and Plymouth proclaimed the twenty-fourth of June as a day for such observance. The date did not fall on Sunday but it was to be kept in exactly the same manner as the rigid Puritan Sabbath. No meals were to be prepared nor work of any kind to be done from sundown on the twenty-third to the same time on the following day. Serv-

ices were to be held morning and afternoon in every meetinghouse in the colonies. Even people who lived at difficult
distances from centers where there was a meetinghouse
were urged to make the journey to some place where they
could attend the meetings and thus unite their prayers
with others.

Free-thinking Rhode Island left people to do as they saw
fit about observing the day but by far the greater number
of the settlements did so.

The Mapes household had never attended public meeting. There had been no Friends meetinghouse in New England until a few years previous and even when that was
established it was too far from their hilltop to be of use to
them. All through the years they had observed the Sabbath at home with the silent service which is the Friends'
way of devotion. So they kept the special day of prayer
in the same manner. In the morning they gathered to sit
for an hour in silent communion with the Spirit. And
again in the afternoon.

They were all so accustomed to the long hours of complete quiet that even the lively Jonathan accepted them
without question. He had been so trained from infancy
that he could slip into a state of complete passivity simply
by closing his eyes. He was not conscious of any great
spiritual revelations at these times such as many folks told
about. But they were quite pleasant. A warm, bright stillness seemed to enfold him which was rather like the stillness of a sunny afternoon when he was fishing on the river
bank. It must be confessed that often during these times
he dozed. He could slip from sleeping to waking and back
again with no outward evidence and no one was the
wiser.

It was warm on that late June day and the hours of fasting inactivity had made him even more drowsy than usual.
During the afternoon sitting he could hardly stay awake
at all. He had dozed so often that even when he wakened
he still felt he was asleep. He thought he was dreaming
that he was talking to Hiram Tufts on his mill; but the
tap-tap-tap of the message was so faint he couldn't make
it out. He rallied his drowsy faculties to a mighty effort
to hear and understand and, in the effort, awakened to the
realization that he was not dreaming after all. He really
was hearing Hiram's mill!

Yet how could that be possible, he argued. The Tufts
were followers of Roger Williams and broad in their views,
but they still held to all the rigid Puritan ways of observing the Sabbath. Certainly on such a special day of religious devotion as this Hiram would never be allowed to use
the mill for idle chatter, and the family would go hungry
rather than use it for pounding meal. Beside, he remembered suddenly, beyond doubt they would have gone somewhere to the prayer meetings. So of course he must be
dreaming. He pinched himself to see if he could feel it.
Yes, he was awake all right—there was no doubt about
that—and Hiram's mill was tap-tapping with stubborn in-
sistence. Surely the others must be hearing it also. He
opened his eyes just a crack and looked sidewise at his
father under lowered lids.

When Joshua sat in the silence he was able to remove
himself utterly from the outer world. At such times his
face looked as though it were molded in wax. There was
never any evidence on it that he was in the least aware
of things going on about him. Now he was sitting with
closed eyes, as silent as usual; but there was a look of at-

tention to some outer thing upon his face.

"He's hearin' it all right," thought Jonathan and shifted his eyes to look at his mother.

She was doing just the same thing he was—looking cautiously about under dropped lids to see if any of the others were hearing the sound.

The boy cast his eyes round to take in his sister. Hannah was making no pretense. She was sitting bolt upright, her eyes wide open, her head lifted in intent listening. So Jonathan opened his eyes too and glanced again at his father.

Joshua's eyes were open also now and resting on the boy with the vague look of one just roused from unconsciousness.

"Son," he asked in a faraway voice, "is that the Tufts' mill I hear?"

Hannah broke in before Jonathan could answer. "Aye, it is, Father. I've been hearing it this long time."

Her father glanced at her, still vague, and then turned back to Jonathan. "Are they pounding meal—can thee tell, son? Or is Hiram trying to say something to thee?"

"Hiram's talking, sir. I'm sure o' that. But in here I can't make out what he's saying."

The vagueness was gone from Joshua's look now. He rose with quick decisiveness. "We'd best go out then. The Tufts would ne'er let Hiram use the mill today except in some dire need. Run on quickly, son, and let him know thee hears. We will come after."

Jonathan dashed off to the barnyard and the others followed as quickly as they could. Mid-way of the garden path Hiram's mill fell silent.

"Oh, dear," cried Hannah, "he's gone."

"He'll try again when he hears our mill," Joshua reassured her. "There," he added as the first sound of their own mill came to them, "Jonathan has started talking now."

By the time they reached the barnyard, the boy had finished sending his brief message to Hiram and was waiting, pestle suspended, for the hoped-for response. In a moment the distant tapping began. The faint sound had a strangely urgent note.

Jonathan's whole body was tense with listening. After the first moment or two of tapping his eyes widened with alarm and as it proceeded the color ebbed from his face leaving his freckles standing out in startling brownness against its pallor.

"What is it, son?" Joshua demanded sharply even before the message came to an end.

But the boy waved a silencing hand at him and they all stood in tense quiet till the sound ceased.

"There's been an Indian raid," he announced when the sound of the last tap died away. "A lot of folks were killed."

No one made any outcry. They just stood there shocked into silence.

Naomi was the first to find her voice. "At the Tufts'?" she asked in a choked voice.

The boy shook his head. "Nay, 'twas somewhere where they'd gone to the prayermeeting. The Indians fell on the folk coming out of the meetinghouse. But Hiram and his father and mother got away to where they had their horse hitched and all piled on together and rode home like sixty. They'd just got there when he started tryin' to tell me."

"But where was the raid?" his father questioned

204

urgently.

Jonathan's face was puckered with distress. "Hiram couldn't tell me. We've ne'er contrived ways of saying places."

Joshua looked helplessly at Naomi. "Where would the Tufts be likely to go to meeting?" he asked. "There are a half dozen villages an equal distance from them."

Naomi considered with drawn brows. "Oh," she cried at length, "where they have folk, of course. That would be Seekonk, where Master Tufts has a sister, or Swanzey, where his wife's brother lives."

"Swanzey seems the most likely place for a raid. 'Tis the nearest village to Mount Hope," Joshua speculated. "Dear, dear," he added, shaking his head with a frown of frustrated distress. "I wish we could make sure."

"I think we might be able to find out, Father," Hannah suggested timidly. Then she turned to Jonathan. "Can thee say 'swan' on the mill, brother?" she asked.

Jonathan looked at her blankly, shaking his head. "We ne'er made up a way to say it. We'd no need to talk of the creatures. There're none hereabout."

Hannah thought a moment. "Well then," she said, "can thee say these words?" She checked them off on her fingers. "Big, white, water, and bird."

Before she finished the boy was nodding eagerly. "Aye, I can say all of those."

Hannah gave him a wan smile. "Then ask Hiram whether the first part of the name of the place where the raid was doesn't sound the same as the name of a big white water bird."

The boy stared at his sister with open admiration for an instant and then started tapping.

A brief answer came back at once.

"He says it does," Jonathan announced when Hiram's mill fell silent. "The one with the long neck."

"Swanzey!" said Joshua. "I thought as much."

They all stood silent again, each trying to grasp the significance of the calamity.

"Is it the start of the uprising folk have been looking to see, Father?" Hannah asked at length.

Joshua gave a heavy sigh. "Who can tell? But it looks much like it."

Jonathan left his mill and came to stand close to his father as though to gather courage from his nearness. "Will they wipe out the English, sir, like they said?"

His father gave vent to an exclamation of emphatic denial. "Counterwise, son, the English will wipe out the Pokanokets and any of the other tribes that take part in the conflict. They'll all go the way of the Pequots." He was silent a little, while an expression of poignant compassion came into his face. "Poor Metacomet, poor misguided creature," he said at length. "He has sealed the doom of his people."

Tears came into Hannah's eyes. "Paucottauwat too? And Qunneke and sweet little Moosquin?" she asked.

Before Joshua could answer Naomi broke in, a tone of distinct disapproval in her voice. "Why think only of the Indians?" she demanded with some bitterness. "What of those poor folk at Swanzey who have had their loved ones massacred today?"

"Oh, dear wife," cried Joshua, "we do think of them with quite the same sorrow as thy own. But 'tis of the final result of the conflict for the two races that I am thinking. And of the two 'tis the red man that is to be pitied. The English will suffer sorely, 'tis true. Hundreds of lives will be lost. Numberless homes—aye, perchance e'en whole villages will be destroyed. Much that we have been building so painfully here in the colonies will be wiped out. But in the end the white race will be victorious. A future unshadowed by the menace of the natives and enriched by possession of their lands lies ahead for us. For the Pokanokets and their allies there is naught but annihilation. The tribes will be scattered. The few tribesmen that escape death or captivity in the conflict may find refuge with other tribes, but their own tribal identity will be lost. The captives will be sold into slavery and live out their lives in bondage." He paused and stood looking sadly into space for a while, then added in a sorrowful voice, "A once proud people will be brought to naught. For them, this is the beginning of the end."

15

THE WHITE FEATHER

WITHIN a few days after the attack at Swanzey the once lonely trail which crossed the Mapes' hilltop had become a teeming thoroughfare. Other more serious raids on villages in Plymouth territory had followed the first attack in rapid succession. At the same time small bands of warriors roved the countryside spreading death and devastation over miles of fertile farmland. The young crops in the fields were destroyed, houses and barns were smoking ruins. Hundreds of homeless and terrified people were fleeing to places holding forth a promise of safety.

No spot in all New England offered such protection as Aquidneck Island. Cut off from the mainland by surrounding waters in which a patrol of armed boats kept constant vigil, it could defy attack completely. So it was to this haven the largest number of the refugees turned their faces, traveling across the Plymouth frontier and Rhode Island by the Pequot Path to Providence, there to seek boats to take them on down Narragansett Bay to the island.

Day and night they came toiling up the Mapes' hillside, carrying their sick and wounded in litters borne on the shoulders of the strongest, laden with children too young to walk and with the few possessions they had been able to save. And one and all they were made welcome in the chandler's house. The sick and wounded were put to bed and nursed with the tenderest care. All were fed and comforted. During the remainder of June and half of July none of the family slept a night in their own beds.

Each newly arrived group brought further reports of what was taking place in the stricken territory. Troops raised by the Plymouth government had already been on their way to Mount Hope to quell the Wampanoag disorders when the Swanzey attack took place. They had arrived the following day. News of the disaster had quickly brought additional troops from Massachusetts. Philip had been driven from his stronghold and a vigorous campaign of counterattack was being waged against the Indian foe, calculated to strike terror to the heart of the boldest warrior.

Later comers had seen some of that warfare and told with evident admiration of the daring and ruthless efficiency of the Puritan fighting men. Hannah felt faint with sick protest as she listened to the accounts of raids upon Indian villages in which the tactics employed seemed no less cruel and horrible than those practiced by the enemy regarded as a savage. Women and children were slain without mercy; old men, youths, and even children were tortured in the effort to wring information of military value from them. All the prisoners taken were being sold as slaves and shipped off to the West Indies.

Joshua was white to the lips, but he held his peace for he knew it would be useless to say anything in dissent. But the statement that prisoners were being sold as slaves brought a pained cry of protest from Hannah. The home village of Paucottauwat's family was in the heart of the invaded country and the thought of the gentle Qunneke and her children being sold into bondage was more than the girl could bear. "I'd far rather they'd been killed," she insisted almost in tears.

Her father tried to calm her with comforting assurances. "They were most like not in their village at all, my dear," he told her, "for beyond doubt Paucottauwat would have sent them to stay with the Narragansetts." He turned to the man who had been doing the talking and explained how it happened the girl felt such an affectionate concern for the Indians.

He looked faintly uncomfortable. "I know," he said. "There are a lot of folks that have friends among the natives. It makes the present trouble a lot harder on 'em." He paused to glance at Hannah with sympathetic concern. "It's to be hoped, really, that the Wampanoags she spoke of aren't with the Narragansetts for it looks like they won't be let stay for long. The commissioners of the colonies are bent on havin' all of them returned as prisoners. A new treaty agreein' to surrender groups of 'em from time to time has just been signed up."

Joshua's brows went up with shocked incredulity. "Thee must be mistaken as to that, my friend. The Narragansetts would ne'er sign such a treaty. For to them as to all the red men the laws of hospitality are sacred."

The other man shrugged. "Laws or no laws, it has been signed sure enough, and do they not live up to it I've a notion the commissioners won't stop at talk."

Hannah saw a faintly ironic smile pass across her father's face and he asked no further regarding the new treaty.

But later when they were alone she questioned him about it.

"Did he mean the English would attack the Narragansetts to get the Wampanoags they have with them?" she asked.

Her father did not give a direct answer. " 'Tis a threat they can hold o'er the tribe, thinking 'twill bring them to terms. But I'm mortal sure a long time will pass ere they can enforce that treaty." He gave a short, amused chuckle. "Whoever drew it up surely knows naught of the subtle workings of an Indian's mind or he would ne'er have phrased it 'from time to time.' For to an Indian that can be construed to mean from now till doomsday."

Evidently he was right, for no Wampanoags were delivered and the matter was not pressed because soon the Puritan colonies had other much more serious matters to engage their attention. In mid-July the Nipmucks and a number of river tribes in the Connecticut River valley went on the warpath also. Philip and his warriors slipped through the fingers of the English troops and, marching rapidly westward across Massachusetts, joined their forces with those of the new allies. The scene of the war was shifted to western Massachusetts and the Connecticut border.

For the time being Plymouth was again at peace and people ceased to leave the district. Few refugees passed now on the trail, for those fleeing the new area of devastation went another way to Providence. Quiet and solitude returned to the Mapes' hilltop once more. They were free to take up the concerns of their own lives again.

And chief among those concerns was the desire to hear from Patrick. While travelers, many of whom were going

direct to Newport, had been passing almost daily it had
been possible to send him letters regularly. But since of all
those who went none were returning, letters from him
could get no farther than Providence. So they had written
him to send letters there at least and when it was possible
Joshua would go in and get them. And now that there
were no refugees to care for, he could do so.

He insisted on going alone, however, because even in a
district presumably at peace travel over a woodland trail
might not prove entirely free of danger. The family
watched anxiously for his return and when Hannah saw
him coming she ran out eagerly to meet him. She noted
at once that there was a different look about him than he
had worn for many months. He moved with a brisk pro-
fessional air and there was an expression of new interest
and satisfaction on his face. She knew without asking that
there had been letters from Patrick, that he had already
read them, and that they contained something of a happy
nature regarding his trade.

She was right. There were several letters. Those written
while the menace of the war had been so close to them
were entirely given up to expressions of concern for them
and further urging that they should come to Newport.
But the last, written since the war had shifted to other
territory, was filled with plans for his coming back to
them for the fall candle making. He had been taking a
part of his pay in spermaceti for many months, he wrote,
and now had enough stored away to make the candles required for their trade. He had been granted leave to go for
two months and was planning to arrive in Providence on
the first of September.

"So," said Joshua in a happy voice as he put the letter

aside, "since I was assured of being able to deliver spermaceti candles to those of my customers that want them, I took time while in Providence to make sure of their orders beforehand. Some few were afraid to order their full supply because of the uncertainties of the war, but on the whole things promise well, and we'll now have our hands full getting ready for the making ere Patrick comes."

Hannah was glad there was plenty of work to be done. It made the days which must go by before Patrick could be with them pass more quickly. August was over before she could have believed it could be—and then, wonder of wonders, Patrick was there. Life was just as it had been a year before during their first candle making together, except that this time it was Patrick who was the teacher when they came to make the spermaceti candles.

Hannah was so happy she had to keep reminding herself she had no right to be so full of joy while such tragic things were happening only a few miles away from them. But, for that matter, all the others were almost equally happy too. Patrick was the only one whose joy was somewhat clouded and that was because he had a problem hanging over him which, through most of his visit, he could not bring himself to mention.

Simon Mercedes had proposed that during the winter he should go on a voyage with one of the whaling vessels which brought the whale oil they used in the shop. Sperm whales swam southward as the cold set in, so in the winter many whaling vessels made voyages into southern waters which took them far from New England and kept them away for periods of many months. At any other time Patrick would have welcomed such an opportunity as a rare adventure. Now the feeling that during those months the war might engulf Rhode Island and he would be unable to get news of Hannah and the rest of his foster family made him loath to consider it. Yet he knew Simon Mercedes had made the suggestion because he felt the experience would go far toward bringing about the possibility of the establishment of the independent business for Joshua toward which the boy was working. For that reason he felt he really ought to go—and between the one feeling and the other he was torn with conflict.

For a time Joshua was unaware of the struggle going on in the boy's mind but as the days went by he could not but note evidences of the strife and finally asked him gently what was troubling him. Patrick had already reached the conclusion the only way to solve the problem was to talk it over with the family and was much relieved to be provided with the opening to lay it before them.

Hannah said nothing but, in spite of herself, her face showed the grief she felt at having him go. Naomi's revealed open opposition to the idea which she was plainly only awaiting an opening to express. But Joshua's expression betrayed nothing but gratification.

"Why, lad, that would be wonderful for thee," he exclaimed when Patrick came to an end. "By all means thee must go. Thee could do no good here in case of trouble."

"But I'd have no way of knowing should aught befall you here," the boy protested.

"Naught will befall us," Joshua answered quietly.

His tone had a kind of calm assurance which made Patrick glance at him with quick question. Someway the boy sensed quite clearly that he had not made the statement simply as a means of giving reassurance. He had given utterance with complete simplicity to a thing he not so much felt as deeply knew to be true. Evidently he saw the question in Patrick's eyes for he answered it before the boy could put it into words.

"I could scarce tell thee how I know that, lad—but I do. Thee will but have to take it on faith." He paused, looking at the boy as though trying to think how he could make him understand. After a moment he went on, " 'Tis with us now as it has e'er been about setting the traveler's candle. That token of trust in our fellowmen made us safe with any who entered our house. So now I know we will be safe so long as our trust in our Indian friends remains unshaken. Go and be at peace about us."

Patrick looked at Hannah for the final answer. Tears were running down her cheeks but she smiled at him with brave assurance. "Father is right," she said simply. "Thee should go."

He accepted her decision without question—as deep in his heart he knew he should always accept any decision she might make for him.

After that, the proposed voyage became an exciting event toward which they could all plan in common. The trip to Providence to deliver the finished candles should be made to coincide with his departure for Newport, they decided, so that it need be made but once. And, because of the present possible dangers of travel, only Joshua would go with him. The day for his departure came, the farewells were said, and the two set off for Providence.

As on the previous year, they went first to Roger Williams. Patrick was shocked to see how he had changed. His years seemed to rest heavily upon him now. Deep lines of fatigue and anxiety were etched on his face. Sorrow and weary discouragement looked out of his kind eyes.

"You catch me barely returned home," he told them after the usual greetings. "I was called upon to try once more to effect some agreement between the Narragansetts and the commissioners of the colonies."

"So?" said Joshua. "I take it then no Wampanoags have been delivered from time to time." There was an ironic emphasis on the final words.

"None," replied their host. "But what else could they expect? The treaty was not e'en signed by Canonchet, the Grand Sachem. Without his mark upon it they cannot hold it binding on the tribes."

"I make no doubt they tried to wring another treaty or fresh promises from the sachem?" said Joshua.

"Aye, they did. But 'twas to no avail. You know the proud bearing of the young prince. He drew himself to all his height and looked at them with royal scorn. 'Not a Wampanoag,' he said, 'nor the paring of a Wampanoag's toenail.' And not all they—or I—could say would shake him."

"Thee?" exclaimed Joshua in a shocked voice. "Thee means thee, too, tried to persuade him to give over the women and children given into the care of his people as a sacred trust?"

Roger Williams leaned back in his chair and let his hands fall limply on his knees, palms upward in a gesture of exhaustion and defeat. "What else could I do, my friend?" he demanded in a flat voice. "Horrible as it seems to give over those innocent, hapless folk, 'tis, I fear, the only way of safety for our own Plantation. You know the Bay Colony as well as I. 'Twill brook no such defiance of its authority. One day 'twill decide to enforce it at the point of the sword—and war will be let loose upon us." He paused looking pleadingly at Joshua as though begging him to understand the motive which had prompted his action. "We must avoid war here so be 'tis in any way possible, not only for the sake of lives both white and red but for the sake of the thing for which the Plantation stands. An Indian uprising would set it back so far that when peace came 'twould be near like starting at the beginning again. And I am an old man now. I would have too few years left to do what would be needed."

Patrick was flooded with incredulous admiration. He would actually start all over again, he marveled—this tired old man! It seemed beyond believing. "But how can you do it, sir?" he found himself demanding before he had time to consider. "How can you keep such faith in being able to work out the things you hoped you might bring to pass, when things like this keep happening to prove how inhumane men are to each other?"

His outburst brought a quizzical, musing smile into the tired eyes. "I sometimes wonder myself," the weary reformer admitted. There was no hint of offense in his voice, and after he had spoken he sat looking at the boy with unseeing eyes for a long moment as though trying to analyze his own incentives. "Vision is a hard master," he said at length with a sigh. "Once a man has clearly seen what may be he can ne'er again abide content in the faulty thing that is." He fell silent again but the gaze which rested on Patrick was deeply aware of him now, penetrating and thoughtful. "I've a notion you'll be the same yourself one day, lad. You have the hatred of wrong which fires in men the passion for right. When the full vision of the good day right may bring comes to you and you learn to trust it, naught will turn you from its service either."

The boy gave a rueful shrug. "I doubt it, sir. There's naught I'd like so much to live to see as the things you spoke of when I was here before; but I've no real trust they'll actually come to pass."

"You will have," said Roger Williams. His voice was quiet but there was such a ring of conviction and prophecy in it that Patrick could not forget its sound. Weeks after when he was out at sea he would wake at night thinking he heard it in the sound of the waves, and lie in his hard, narrow bunk wondering.

Off at sea he did not know that events in New England soon proved Roger Williams right in other prophecies he had made. Canonchet's haughty reply to the commissioners aroused exactly the response in Massachusetts he had feared. In November they met in Boston and, without further parley, drew up a proclamation which was practically a declaration of war upon the Narragansetts. The largest army ever raised in New England was mustered. In December it marched into Rhode Island.

Its destination was the tribal fortress of the Narragansetts, the fortified village near Pettyquamscott to which Wattanho had gone for his training. But on the march through Narragansett territory, all the villages through which the troops passed were destroyed and their food stores confiscated. At dawn on December nineteenth a surprise attack on the fortress was made. Over two hundred warriors were killed or wounded in its defense; but, by sunrise, every wigwam had been set afire and numbers of old men, women, and children had perished in the flames. All its winter food supply was destroyed. The inhabitants that survived were homeless and destitute.

Rhode Island waited terrified for the Narragansetts to retaliate by going on the warpath. Instead the chiefs began a series of efforts to make peace. They did not want to make war on the white race, they insisted. Especially not on Rhode Island. They had no quarrel with their neighbors. They asked for a truce in order that terms of a new treaty might be discussed. It was granted gladly, for the English troops had also lost heavily in the attack on the fortress and provisions for the army were nearly exhausted. Hostilities were suspended and negotiations dragged on through two months, both sides glad of a respite from fighting during the bitterest winter weather. But no agreement was reached in the end. No Wampanoags were surrendered and without that Massachusetts would not rest satisfied. The truce was ended. Against their will and better judgment the Narragansetts were at war.

But their initial attack was not upon Rhode Island. Canonchet and his warriors marched rapidly northwestward and joined Philip's forces. The reinforcements brought renewed strength to the war-weary Wampanoags. The conflict took on new impetus. The tide of terror turned eastward and swept nearly to Boston, back into Plymouth and finally on into Rhode Island.

The horrors of Indian warfare came nearer and nearer to the Mapes' hilltop. Refugees were passing on the trail again but few stayed for the night. All that could possibly manage the few miles more went on to Pawtucket to take shelter behind the thick walls of the fort made from Master Jenks' iron mill. Many tried earnestly to persuade Joshua and his family to go with them. At first none of them would consider the idea at all; but at length Naomi began to weaken. The day came at last when concern for her children outweighed every other consideration.

She drew Joshua into their bed-chamber and closed the door. "Let us go to the fort, husband," she urged. " 'Tis well enough for us to face danger, but we've no right to put our children in jeopardy."

"I've been thinking the same myself," he admitted. "Thee and the children must go before night. I will stay to set the candle."

Naomi gave a sharp cry of protest. "Nay, nay, husband! We have faced all our bitter trials together. I could not leave thee e'en for the children's sake. So be thee is bent on staying, I must also."

Joshua's face was drawn with conflict. "For myself I know I am right to stay. But thee and the children should not unless each had a deep inner knowing like my own."

"My knowing is so clouded with fears I cannot trust it now," Naomi acknowledged unhappily. "As to the children, I've no way of knowing how they feel, for they would not say unless we did. Let us put the matter to a vote, as is the way of our people, and abide by the will of the majority."

"Thee would be content with that?" asked Joshua with great relief.

Naomi hesitated a moment. "I think so, husband," she answered doubtfully. She put her hand into Joshua's. "Let us go now and tell the others," she added.

"Before we vote," Joshua continued after he had told Hannah and Jonathan what they had decided, "let us each seek the guidance of the Inner Voice. Then we will be sure we have chosen according to the Great Will."

They stood silent a few moments, then Joshua opened

220

his eyes and turned them upon Naomi with tender question.

"Well, wife?" he said gently.

Naomi's face had a stricken look and her voice faltered like a penitent child's. "I—I—I cannot help it, husband. I vote to go."

Joshua gave her a comforting smile and turned to Hannah.

"Well, daughter?" he said again.

Even Hannah's lips were white, but the hazel eyes were steady and as clear as untroubled pools. Before answering she put her arm about her mother as though hoping thus to make what she was about to say easier for her. "I vote to stay, Father," she said low and clear. "I think we should."

Her father's eyes thanked her before they passed on to Jonathan.

The boy stood very straight, his sturdy legs apart and his head held high as though in defiance of fear. "Me too," he answered stoutly. "The Indians won't hurt us."

Joshua gathered the boy to him. "Well said, son," he said with a little choke in his voice. "That's as I think, too." He looked regretfully at his wife. "Thee knows my vote without my giving it, my dear. We are three to thy one. Can thee content thyself with that?"

Naomi nodded, biting her lips. "Since you all vote that way it must be the right thing for us to stay, and I'll try to trust that all will be well."

But there was still another trial for her to meet. Neighbors passed on their way to the fort just at dusk and stopped to tell them a small band of Indians had been seen lurking in the woods at the foot of their hill. Naomi stood firm in her acceptance of the decision to stay, but when it came time to set the traveler's candle she begged that for just that one night they should let it go unlighted. " 'Twould guide those Indians right to our door," she pointed out. "Without it our house might pass unnoticed in the dark."

Hannah and Jonathan were standing waiting for their parts in the little evening ceremony. Joshua turned to them.

"What do you think, children?" he asked.

Jonathan spoke up at once for setting the candle; but having voted against her mother before it seemed more than Hannah could do to do so again. "Mother may be right," she admitted doubtfully. She stood looking away with that expression of farseeing she sometimes had. And gradually certainty came into her face. "Nay," she said at last with great decision, "we should set the candle. We have stayed to do that, and do we fail in that we will have failed in all."

Then as though by a miracle, Naomi's fears seemed to drop from her. "Of course we should set it," she said with definiteness equal to Hannah's. "I was confused by my fears for you children, but now I see plain again."

So they set the candle, once more united in thought, and went to their beds.

In spite of the stand she had taken, Hannah could not quite put fear from her altogether. She could not go to sleep but lay stiff in her bed, listening, listening, her ears strained for the slightest sound. The hours slipped slowly by. Through the cracks in the shutters of the tiny window in the gable, she could see that the full moon had crossed the heavens and was close to setting over the western hill.

She gave a sigh of relief—that meant the night was more than half gone. Then suddenly she sat up in bed, catching her breath. She was certain she heard stealthy footsteps in the dooryard. She waited in an agony of listening. The slow minutes passed in deathly silence. Nothing happened. At length she could stand the suspense no longer, and slipping out of bed crept to the window hole to peep out. The moon was just setting behind the western hill, gilding its top with shimmering light. Below that faint circle of light, the hillslope, their own hilltop, and all the surrounding hills were in utter darkness. She could see nothing because of it. Then, out of the darkness, a line of shadowy figures emerged into the light of the hilltop and slipped across it, standing out, one by one, in sharp silhouette as they passed across the moon. There was no doubt about it—they were Indians.

The last figure passed. The moon sank slowly out of sight. The world seemed swallowed up in silent blackness.

The girl crept back to bed and lay wondering. Why had they come and gone like that? The slow march of dragging moments began again. Presently she sat up once more in surprise. She must have dozed, after all, and morning was coming, for light showed through the cracks of the shutters. Then, as she watched, she knew with terrible certainty it was not the blessed light of day. She leaped out of bed and, running to the window, threw the shutter wide. The whole sky beyond the western hill was alight with an angry red glare.

"The mill!" she whispered. "They're burning the defensible house."

She watched till the glare died away and then crept back to bed. For a long time she was too shaken with horror for

223

their neighbors who must have been there to think of herself or her own family. But suddenly the thought came,
"Why, had we gone as Mother wished, we would have been
there too." She sat up in bed and bowed her head on her
knees as realization came. They had voted to stay, they had
trusted, and they had been safe. Quiet and a sense of complete security enfolded her. She lay down and soon was fast
asleep.

It was full daylight when she woke. She dressed hastily
and when she went downstairs she found her father and
Jonathan already at the table eating. Her father greeted
her with a finger raised as a warning for quiet.

"Thy mother is still sleeping," he told her. "She did not
sleep much through the night and we'll let her sleep till
she wakens now."

"I scarce slept at all either, Father," she answered and
went on to tell him what she had seen.

He rose from the table at once. "Let us go out and look
about," he said. "We saw the flames but naught else."

They found nothing at first, but presently in a spot soft
with the late March thaw Jonathan discovered tracks
plainly made by moccasined feet. But that was all and they
were on their way in again when Jonathan stopped on the
door-stone pointing above the door-frame.

"Look, Father," he cried, "there's a feather stuck in
there that wasn't there last night."

Joshua gave a little exclamation, reached up, and took it
down. It was a long white quill like the one Paucottauwat
had worn in his hair knot. He stood looking at it, his face
flooded with deep feeling and gratitude. A small square of
birch bark was attached to it and as he turned it over a
glad cry escaped him. There were a dozen or so lines

scratched upon it which were evidently meant as a drawing of a large, antlered animal.

"It looks like a deer," said Jonathan.

The chandler's eyes were glowing. "It is a deer," he said, "the Great Deer."

"Paucottauwat!" cried Hannah. "It was he who was here last night. He left the feather to let us know he passed."

"Nay, more, my child," her father told her. "He came on purpose to place it there. A white feather set above the door is a token among the Indians that the house where it is placed shall be inviolate from attack." He paused and stood looking away to the hills, his face soft with tenderness. "He kept his pledge in his own way after all," he said softly. "He did not forget."

Hannah slipped her hand timidly into his. "Father," she said in a hushed voice, "had we not placed the candle, he would not have known what house was ours."

Joshua nodded. He was far beyond words. The answer to his trust was almost too great a miracle. He replaced the little guardian of their safety above the door and they all stood looking up with reverent eyes at that small but potent token of unbroken trust.

16

A LIGHT SET UPON A HILL

A FEW days after the burning of the defensible house at Pawtucket, Patrick sailed back into New England waters happily ignorant of the recent tragedy. Away at sea he had received no news from Rhode Island and was returning in specially high spirits because his voyage had proved successful beyond his wildest hopes. He was bearing assurances for Joshua which would make the future of his trade secure. And the best part of it was that the good fortune could be, in a sense, attributed to Joshua's influence rather than Patrick's efforts.

Simon Mercedes had selected the captain with whom the boy was to sail with far-sighted wisdom, and prepared for their meeting with astute understanding of human nature. He had told Patrick nothing of the man except that his name was Thomas Dexter and he came from New Bedford. Patrick had heard a good deal about the place, for much of the oil they used in the shop came from there. He knew it was located on Buzzards Bay and was fast coming to be one of the most important whaling stations in the colonies. But he had not chanced to learn one fact about it which, under the circumstances, would have been of very great interest to him. A number of its most prominent whalers were Quakers. Thomas Dexter was one of them—and Simon Mercedes had shrewdly selected him for that reason.

Patrick's exclamation of pleased surprise when his new captain addressed him with the familiar "thee" served as a peculiarly fortunate introduction. An explanation of why he was so delighted to find himself associated with a Quaker naturally followed and that, of course, involved an enthusiastic account of his association with Joshua. The glowing picture he painted of the Quaker chandler would have won respect and admiration for him from any listener. So when in due course the boy told the story of Joshua's difficulties because of the introduction of spermaceti candles in Newport, the prosperous Quaker whaler was more than ready to give a sympathetic ear and to desire to be helpful. In addition he knew enough of the whaling industry to foresee the financial possibilities of a venture in making spermaceti candles and was not averse to having a share in it. As a result of this happy combination of circumstances, before the voyage was over he had proposed that he would finance such a venture and engage to provide the necessary spermaceti and whale oil in return for a small interest in the business.

Patrick's cup of joy was full to the brim. He felt he could see the realization of his dreams coming true. Before long his vision of that enticing sign, "Mapes and Mapes; Candle Chandlers," would be a reality! He stood at the ship's rail, as it sailed into Narragansett Bay to dock at Newport, glowing with triumph and filled with an almost uncontrollable eagerness to reach the Mapes' hilltop and pour out his happy news. The very next morning before sunup he would be off on his journey thither, he told himself.

But as they came in sight of the town its appearance smote him with apprehension. The hillsides above and about it were covered almost solidly with hastily constructed shelters. Strand Street was swarming with people. As the ship drew alongside the wharf he saw it was crowded with excited men, and as soon as they were within earshot some of them began shouting out the news.

An attack upon Providence had taken place only two days before, following close on the burning of most of the settlement of Pawtucket. Half of Providence had been burned also and a large part of its population had taken refuge in Newport. Warwick was wiped out altogether and practically the entire district between the Plymouth seaboard and Narragansett Bay had been laid waste.

Patrick bent his head onto his folded arms on the boat rail and groaned aloud. That tide of devastation had swept over the Mapes' hilltop. Beyond doubt they must have perished in it.

A gentle touch on his shoulder made him look up to see Captain Dexter beside him. "Thee must not give way thus, my boy," he urged. "There's good hope thy friends may be here with all the rest in Newport."

Hope dawned in Patrick's eyes. "Why, so they might be," he agreed with huge relief. "I'd not thought of that." Then as his gaze roved over the crowded streets and hillsides, discouragement came into his face again. "But how am I to find them amid all these people?" he added in a disheartened voice.

"The Friends Master Mapes knew here would know should they be in the town. Do thee go seek them while I visit my own family. By God's grace they were safe here through this terror, for I brought them hither during the first trouble in Plymouth. I will join thee at Simon Mercedes' in an hour. Should thee have found out nothing, then we will all set forth upon search of the town."

Patrick hurried off hopefully; but none of Joshua's Quaker acquaintances had heard of him. He returned to the shop convinced the Mapes were not in Newport. Nevertheless, he would not give up until every one of the refugee shelters had been canvassed and every possible clue run to earth. By the second night he knew it was hopeless.

"On the morrow I shall find a boat to take me to Providence and push on to their hill from there," he announced desperately.

Simon Mercedes and Captain Dexter both protested violently.

"Why, boy, thee would ne'er reach the place alive. The woods between Pawtucket and their hill are beyond doubt still infested with Indians," declared the Captain.

"But I must get there," insisted Patrick.

"I think there will be a way," said Simon Mercedes quietly. "I heard today that some troops from Massachusetts are on their way to Rhode Island. They'd no doubt be going to Pawtucket, and could you manage to join them somewhere near the coast in Plymouth you could make the journey safely with them." He glanced questioningly at Captain Dexter. "You would take the boy to Plymouth by ship, would you not, Captain?"

"To be sure," he replied. "I was intending to sail for Bedford in a day or so in any case, to see how things fared there. 'Twould be little to go on to Plymouth."

A few days later Patrick had reached Plymouth, learned

the probable whereabouts of the militia on its way to Rhode Island, and in spite of Captain Dexter's protests had set off alone to try to catch up with it.

His way led through the same stretch of country he had crossed after his escape from the slave ship. He had not seen it since that day, and though the blackened villages and devastated fields bore little semblance to the fertile and thriving countryside it had been then, there were still many landmarks which brought poignant remembrances of his feelings on that trip. Even in his present state of desperate anxiety he realized what a different boy he was now from that bitter, hopeless lad filled with hard disbelief in all mankind and hot hatred for men's evil ways. The change had come so gradually he had not been aware of it. But now, in a flash of vision, he saw the new boy who was Patrick Mapes. Remembrance of that day in the barnyard, when he had felt Hannah was seeing him as he would sometime be, came over him. "But now that I'm as she'd hoped to see me she may not be alive to see me at all," he groaned.

In his revulsion from the conflicts of warring faiths he had long since turned from anything like prayer. But that thought was too terrible to be borne alone. He had to reach out to some Power greater than himself. "Oh, let her be safe," he whispered in passionate petition, "please, please, let her be safe."

Just after dark he found the militia encamped for the night and with it a number of people who, like himself, were availing themselves of military protection to make the trip into Rhode Island. That was the last full night of rest they had. For from there on no one was inclined to stop longer than was absolutely necessary. They snatched brief rests when it was too dark to follow the trail. The remainder of the time, day or night, they pushed rapidly forward. In a much shorter time than Patrick's original trip had taken they were within a day's march of the Mapes' hilltop.

But that morning a cold storm set in. Rain and hail and flurries of snow hindered their progress. By late afternoon they had only got as far as the beginning of the last stretch of woods that lay between them and the Mapes' hill. The ruins of a farm stood there with enough of the barn still standing to offer shelter from the storm. A vote was taken and the majority was for stopping. But Patrick would not consider it. The night of uncertainty so near his journey's end would have been too terrible an agony to him. So, regardless of the disapproval of the militia commander, he insisted on going on.

Dark shut down before he got through the woods and emerged into the clearing at the foot of the Mapes' hill. He remembered the exact spot at which he had looked up that other stormy night and seen the Mapes' candle shining like a star at the top of the hill. Now he would not let himself look until he came to that place. But when he reached it his courage failed him. If the hilltop was dark he would know they were not there. For a long moment he stood with bent head, steeling himself to that dread possibility, then slowly raised it and turned eager, searching eyes to the hilltop. There was no light shining above it.

A low moan broke from him. It was really just what he had expected—yet he had let himself hope. He was shaken by a convulsion, half sobs, half bitter laughter. "Hope!" he mocked, "a fool's refuge! That and trust. Master Mapes trusted—and now look. A fine end to all the noble talk of having faith in one's fellow man!"

He stood there in the dark with the rain beating on his upturned face and cast to the wind that buffeted him all he had gained since he had stood there before. From now on he would trust nothing, believe nothing. Then he would be safe from hurt.

He would go on and confirm his fears, then he would come back and join with the militia to fight against the people Joshua had taught him to regard as neighbors. He started forward, his eyes on the hilltop. Then suddenly he stopped with a cry. There was a flicker of light in the darkness above it. He stood fairly holding his breath till the flicker became a steady light shining like a star. There was no doubting what it was. It was the traveler's candle!

Sobbing, laughing, panting, he charged up the hill. Stumbling, falling, picking himself up again, and running on till he stood before the house. The blessed little house with its tiny lighted window and its comfortable thatched roof! Nothing was harmed. Everything was just as it had been when he saw it last. It seemed beyond belief!

He was about to burst in at the door when he recalled that now the family would be standing in their silent prayer for travelers. So instead he opened it with caution, stepped softly inside, and closed it noiselessly behind him.

There they stood just as he had seen them so often, the flickering light of the candle falling on their bent heads and quiet faces. Hannah was facing him and it went through him like a knife to see how thin and wan she was. Her face seemed almost transparent and the light of her inner being seemed shining through the delicate flesh almost as though it were glass.

He was sure he had made no sound but presently, just

234

as though he had spoken, the girl raised her head and opened her eyes directly upon him. She made no sound or movement. He saw her give just one sharp intake of breath and then she stood there utterly still, her eyes wide and glowing, pouring out a flood of light and feeling that bridged the space between them and united them more closely than any nearness.

He had no idea how long they stood thus. It might have been an instant—it might well have been an eternity, so much was crowded into that moment. Then evidently something in the atmosphere communicated itself to Naomi, for Patrick heard her gasp. Then her voice rang out in a glad cry.

The next moment they were all about him and he was pouring out the story of his fright about them, his search in Newport, and the horrible moment at the foot of their hill when he had looked up and found their hilltop dark.

"Aye," said Joshua, "we were late with the candle to-night. We were sitting in silence and had not noted that the dark had fallen." Then he in turn told the story of Paucottauwat's visit and their miraculous escape. "So you see, lad," he added softly, "my trust in Paucottauwat was justified. He remembered his pledge and we are safe. 'Tis a testimony I'll ne'er forget. I have seen a miracle. Naught can e'er shake my trust again."

Patrick felt his face burning with shame. How easily his little trust had been shaken! How quick he had been to swear he would trust no more!

As usual Naomi was the first to think of practical matters, to ask when he had eaten last, and to insist on preparing him a good hot meal. While he ate they bridged the gap of absence with a running stream of talk. But Patrick did not tell the great news with which he had been bursting when he arrived in Newport. Some way now it did not seem important.

By the time he had finished eating, it was later than the hour at which the family usually went to their beds. Tonight none of them had any desire to sleep. Joshua mended the fire and they made themselves comfortable about the hearth. There was little talk now. For long stretches they sat in happy silence, resting in the blessed sense of all being together again.

There was no sound but the light purr of the fire and the rustle of the rain on the thatch. And within himself also Patrick felt a great stillness. All his doubts were awed into silence. Here they sat safe amid devastation—more secure than others had been in a fortress. For a time the thought held his mind hushed with wonder, then quietly it unfolded to the truth. They *were* in a fortress—a fortress built of trust. Deep in himself he gave the thought reverent recognition. He, too, had seen a miracle.

After a time Joshua asked some question about his voyage. He answered it and then, at last, went on to tell the news of Captain Dexter's proposal. But even as he did so he could not recapture his previous feeling of excitement about it. Before he was hardly done speaking he broke off with a rueful little laugh. "When I was sailing home it seemed so great a thing I could scarce wait to get here to tell it," he said, "but now it seems like naught."

Joshua gave him a smile of commendation and comfort tinged with wistful regret. "And so it would have been a great thing, lad, had not all this ruin come upon us. Later, perchance, we may be able to take advantage of it. But as things are now, no man with a right mind could think of his own advancement. For many years to come, I fear, we will have to give the best we have to the task of rebuilding what has been destroyed. So many of our strongest have been taken from us, those that are left will have to do duty for a score."

The mention of rebuilding made Patrick think of their last talk with Roger Williams and he asked quickly if Joshua had heard news of him.

"Not yet," Joshua replied, "but I'm near certain he'd be safe. His friendship with the natives would make him so. Should he not be though," he added, "all the more reason we must rebuild so his work can live on."

"Of course," said Patrick with complete and quiet agreement.

He knew now with deep certainty that the Plantation where the experiment in granting freedom of thought and tolerance to all was being made must live on at all hazards. It was "a light set upon a hill for doubting souls to see." That light must be kept aflame till the darkness of oppression had been dispelled. He must give his service to that, just as Roger Williams said he would. He could do it for he could trust now. He had seen a miracle.

He could work for the future even if he never saw any of the fruits of his labor. He was glad he was so young. There was so much to do. A lifetime was not enough; but he would do what he could, content in the knowledge that when the great things Roger Williams had started in Providence came to bless the lives of men everywhere, he would have helped a little to bring them to pass. He, the bitter, hopeless boy to whom the Plantation had given a new life—he, Patrick Mapes.

THE END